'But—marriage... I can't believe you're even suggesting we—'

'Oh, but this isn't a suggestion,' Rico corrected. 'This is what we will do.'

'You can't order me to marry you.' She gave an incredulous laugh. 'You can't drag me up the aisle screaming, Rico.'

'There will be no aisle. There will be no church. I think a quick, discreet service would be more appropriate.'

'You really think you've got it all worked out, don't you?'

'Of course. And when making this decision there is one other thing you need to consider. If you are having my baby, this marriage will be for ever.'

Carol Marinelli is a nurse who loves writing. Or is she a writer who loves nursing? The truth is, Carol's having trouble deciding at the moment—but writing definitely seems to be taking precedence! She's happily married to an eternally patient husband, and mother to three fabulously boisterous children. Add a would-be tennis player, an eternal romantic and a devout daydreamer to the list and that pretty much sums Carol up. Oh, she's also terrible at housework!

Carol also writes for Medical Romance™!

Mama Mia!

Italian Husbands
They're tall, dark…and ready to marry!

There'll be another story
in this great new mini-series…*pronto!*

THE SICILIAN'S BOUGHT BRIDE

BY
CAROL MARINELLI

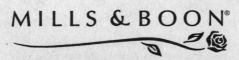

MILLS & BOON®

First published in Great Britain 2004
Harlequin Mills & Boon Limited,
Eton House, 18-24 Paradise Road, Richmond, Surrey TW9 1SR

© Carol Marinelli 2004

ISBN 0 263 83778 5

Set in Times Roman 10½ on 12½ pt.
01-1004-48838

Printed and bound in Spain
by Litografía Rosés, S.A., Barcelona

CHAPTER ONE

'THEY wouldn't have suffered.'

'Of course they wouldn't have.' Catherine could hear the bitterness in her own voice, see the flicker of confusion in the young nurse's expression, but she was too raw, too exhausted, and frankly too damn angry to soften the blow, to spare anyone's feelings.

'My sister and her husband refused to suffer anything. Why worry when you can have a drink? Why dwell on your problems when there's always family to bail you out?' She shook her head fiercely, pressing her fingers against her eyeballs and trying to quell the scream that seemed to be building up inside her.

She knew the poor nurse didn't have a clue what she was going on about, that she was just trying to be kind and say the right thing, and that the car accident had happened in an instant, that it had been over for Marco and Janey before the skidding vehicle had even halted—but her words simply weren't helping. Instead they were touching nerves so raw that every last word made Catherine flinch as she tried and failed not to envisage the final moments of her sister's short life.

Maybe later, Catherine told herself, taking deep breaths and trying to calm herself. Maybe later, when she could think straight—maybe in a few weeks—those words might bring some comfort. But sitting alone in the hospital interview room, exhausted and shellshocked, trying to fathom all that had happened, they brought no comfort at all.

'I really am sorry.' The nurse handed her a small manila envelope and Catherine held on to it tightly, feeling the hard shape of the metal inside it.

'So am I.' The bitterness had gone from her voice now, and Catherine gave the nurse a small nod of thanks. 'You've all been wonderful.'

'Is there anything else I can do for you?'

Catherine shook her head, couldn't even manage an answer, and again she was left alone. Tearing the brown paper, she slid out the contents, staring curiously dry-eyed at the three pieces of jewellery in her palm, tracing the outline of each precious piece as every one told its story. An awful sense of *déjà-vu* descended as she eyed the solitaire diamond ring Janey wore, that had belonged to their mother—the same ring that had slid out of an envelope and into her hand eight years ago. But familiarity brought no comfort. The crash that had killed her parents and the lessons it had taught offered no barrier to the pain she felt now.

It was actually eight years and two months ago, to be precise.

Eight years and two months since she had been handed her parents' belongings along with more responsibility than any nineteen-year-old deserved. But the endless meetings with solicitors and accountants as they attempted to unscramble the chaos her parents had left in their wake had been the easy part.

Dealing with a wayward sixteen-year-old—her sister Janey—had proved the greater feat.

Catherine stared at the ring for a long moment and suddenly she was back there, standing at her mother's dressing table, wishing her thick, dark, curly hair could be as smooth and as straight as her mother's and Janey's, wishing her solemn brown eyes could sparkle blue like theirs.

Instead she had inherited her father's looks—his personality too.

Well, most of it. She was serious, studious, yet she wasn't weak as her father had been, didn't cave in the way he had. One giggle from their mother, one tiny pout of her pretty mouth and John Masters had been lost—would agree to whatever his lovely Lily wanted to put the smile back on her face.

And Janey had been the same—she had possessed the certainty that her looks would get her whatever she had wanted, the same take it or leave it attitude that had held men intrigued, the same inner confidence that someone would always pick up the pieces of the chaos she created—and up till now it had worked.

The glint of the massive sapphire that caught her eye next reminded Catherine so much of her sister's blue eyes that for a second it hurt, physically hurt, to hold the engagement ring Janey had worn with such glee. She had been sure it was her ticket to the fast lane, an end to the financial mess she had got herself into, a way out of the problems that had been just too big for Catherine to sort out this time, however hard she tried.

'Marco's amazing!' Catherine could hear Janey's dizzy, slightly breathless voice as clearly as if she were in the room now. 'Oh, Catherine, you should see where he lives. It's right on the beach—and when I say on the beach, I mean it's literally on it. You step out of the patio and on to the sand. His garage alone is as big as your flat.'

Catherine couldn't have cared less what size Marco's garage was, but she had let Janey ramble for a while, listened to her excited chatter, hoping that it would calm her, that if she let her go on for long enough the euphoria might somehow wear off and that she could find out some more important answers.

'What does he do?' When Janey didn't answer she pushed further. 'For a living—what does Marco do?'

Janey gave a small shrug, tossed her hair and poured herself a drink.

'He has fun.' There was an edge to Janey's voice, a defiant look in her eyes as she stared at her older sister. 'His mother died when he was a teenager,' Janey explained, but without a hint of compassion. 'Just as ours did; only the difference is Bella Mancini actually left something for her children...'

'You mean she left money!' Catherine's voice held a warning ring. Lily might not have been the most conventional mother, but her love of life and her passion for her children had left a void that could never be filled, and no amount of inheritance would have lessened the pain of losing her.

For Catherine at least.

'Oh, spare me the speeches,' Janey spat. 'I don't want to hear again how money isn't important. I don't want to hear again how you worked two jobs while you went through teacher training college—but didn't mind a bit just as long as we were together. If our parents hadn't forgotten to pay their life insurance premiums you wouldn't have had to work so hard. You wouldn't have had to sell the family home and move into a pokey little flat...'

'I didn't mind,' Catherine insisted.

'Well, I did,' Janey snapped, her eyes narrowing. 'I hated being poor and I have no intention of spending the rest of my life chewing my nails over bills. Marco can look after me now, the same way his mother looked after him. Bella Mancini was a property developer, and when she died the business went to her children.'

A flash of recognition offered a ray of hope. The Mancini empire! Oh, Catherine wasn't exactly into reading the business pages of the newspaper, but even without a shred of business acumen she'd have needed to live in a cave for the last decade not to know about the Mancini empire and the stranglehold it held on the Melbourne property market.

The drive along Port Phillip Bay was littered with their latest acquisitions—the smart navy signs telling anyone who cared to see, that this bayview property was being developed by Mancini's.

To make it in the cut-throat world of property development would take stamina, intelligence and, dare she even say it, responsibility. Which, Catherine realised, were the very things Janey needed in a man to keep her on the straight and narrow.

'So Marco's into property development? He's part of the Mancini chain?' Catherine asked, trying not to sound too keen. She had learnt long ago that her approval was the kiss of death for any of Janey's relationships. But the hope that Janey's latest boyfriend might actually posses a scrap of responsibility was doused as quickly as it flared.

'Marco's sold his share of the business to his brother Rico,' Janey corrected, with a note of irritation that Catherine refused to acknowledge. She was determined to find out more about the man Janey was involved with, and was liking him less with each revelation. 'When Marco turned eighteen he was all set to go on board, but by then Rico had decided that he wanted to ''grow'' the business, to work sixty-hour weeks—'

'That's what people do, Janey,' Catherine interrupted, but Janey tossed her blonde hair and took another slug of her wine.

'Why?' she asked, with a glint of challenge in her eyes. 'Why would you bother when you've already made it? Marco's rich in his own right; he doesn't need to work and so he doesn't—it's as simple as that.'

'So he lives off his inheritance?' Catherine shook her head, bewildered. 'He's never even had a job?'

'You sound just like his brother,' Janey sneered. 'And I'll tell you the same thing Marco tells Rico. He doesn't sponge off his family; the money is his to spend.'

'But what sort of a man—?'

'Oh, what would you know about men?' Janey spat back spitefully, 'Who are you to give me advice?'

'I'm your sister.' Cheeks flaming, she had tried to keep her voice even, determined not to rise to the venom that appeared every time she tried to reel Janey in. 'I care about you, Janey, and whether you like it or not I'm concerned about you. Since Mum and Dad...' Her voice trailed off for a second. She didn't want to rake up the past, didn't want to go over those painful memories, but knew that now it was called for. 'I've done my best for us, Janey. I've tried as hard as I can to be there for you, and I'm asking you to listen to me now. I just think it's all too soon. You've only known this Marco for a couple of months. Why are you rushing into things? Why not wait a while and see how things—?'

'I'm pregnant.'

The words were enough to still Catherine, enough to shed a whole new different light on the rumblings of their argument. But even though the news had floored her Catherine deliberately didn't look shocked; she even managed to bite her tongue as Janey took a long sip of wine, knowing now wasn't the time for a lecture.

'Then I'm here for you,' she said again. 'We can sort this out, Janey. Just because you're pregnant it doesn't mean you have to marry him. You don't have to do anything you don't want to do.'

'You really are stupid, aren't you?' The sneer on Janey's pretty face was like a slap to Catherine's cheek. 'For a schoolteacher you really are thick—do you know that? As if I'd get knocked up by *accident*.'

'Knocked up?'

'Pregnant.' Janey gave a malicious laugh. 'Don't think for one moment, Catherine, that I don't know what I'm doing. Don't for one second think that this baby is an accident.'

'Janey, I'm sorry.' Catherine stood up. 'I wasn't suggesting you don't want your baby. I just never thought you…' She struggled helplessly for a second. 'You've never shown any interest in babies.'

'And I don't intend to start.' Janey's eyes narrowed spitefully. 'Do I really have to spell this out, Catherine? I've never had it so good. I can go into a shop, *any* shop— and not look at the price tags. I can walk into the best restaurants without checking the prices. And if you think I'm going to let it end then you don't know me at all.

Maybe Marco does love me, maybe this would have carried on indefinitely, but I'm not prepared to take the risk. So I've created my own little insurance policy.' She patted her stomach, but without a trace of tenderness, laughing mirthlessly at Catherine's shocked expression. 'And if you're worried about my lack of maternal instincts, then don't waste your time; Marco can afford the best nannies. I won't have to do a thing. So you can save the big sister lectures, save the boring speeches—because I don't need you, Catherine.'

Even a year later the words hurt.

The shiny cool gold of Janey's wedding band held its own batch of memories—only this time they weren't exclusive to Janey.

Rico, smart in his dark suit, pausing a fraction too long before handing the rings over, his hand hovering over the Bible before dropping them down in an almost truculent gesture. For Catherine had come the welcome realisation that she wasn't alone in her doubts about this union...

'How are you doing?'

The nurse was back, providing a welcome break from her painful memories, and Catherine gave a tired smile, standing on legs that felt like jelly and smoothing down her skirt as she picked up her jacket.

'I'm fine, but I think I'd like to go to the children's ward and sit with Lily.'

Lily.

A wave of bile threatened to choke her as she thought of her niece, orphaned and alone in the children's ward, and for a moment she wrestled with a surge of hatred—hatred for her sister that was surely out of place now she was dead.

'They said they'd call down when they were ready. It shouldn't be too much longer. I know you must be exhausted, dealing with all this on your own, but at least we've finally managed to locate Marco's parents. Apparently they're holidaying in the States; that's why it's taken so long.'

'His father and stepmother,' Catherine corrected. 'His mother died a long time ago.'

'Well, they've been contacted.'

Catherine gave a weary nod. She hadn't expected the Mancinis to drop everything, and even though she knew a lot needed to be organised and a lot of choices needed to be made, secretly she was relieved nothing would be done tonight.

Tonight was hard enough.

'Someone called Rico's coming, though; he rang on his mobile and said for you to wait here... Are you all right, Miss Masters?' Catherine could see the nurse's mouth moving, the concern in her face as Catherine swayed slightly.

'I'm fine. It's just...' Her pulse seemed to be pounding in her temples and her tongue was dry as she ran it over her lips. Legs that had just found their bearings seemed to be collapsing beneath her again as the nurse pulled the chair nearer and guided Catherine into it.

'Take some slow, deep breaths, Miss Masters, and keep your head down. That's the way. You're just a bit dizzy, that's all, which isn't surprising after all you've been through. I'll get you some water. Just wait there. It's all been such a shock for you it isn't any wonder you're feeling faint.'

Catherine gave a weak nod, burying her head in her

hands and feeling a vague stab of guilt at the nurse's kindness.

Today hadn't really been a shock.

It was agony. It hurt more than she could even begin to bear. But the nurse was wrong again. The sad end to these lives hadn't been a shock. The way Marco and Janey had lived their lives, flaunting society's rules, sure that money would protect them, that rules didn't somehow apply to them…today had been inevitable.

It wasn't the accident and its aftermath that had caused her near-faint—although, Catherine admitted, it would certainly have contributed to it—it wasn't even the long interviews with social workers, trying to map out a tentative path for Lily, and it had very little to do with the fact she hadn't eaten since breakfast. It was all down to the fact that Rico was coming. After all these months she was finally going to see him.

'Rico,' she whispered his name out loud, dragging in the stuffy hospital air and closing her eyes, allowing her mind to drift away for a slice of time, drift away from this awful room and the awful day to the beauty she had once witnessed. The horrors of the days receded as his face came into focus—a face she had pushed out of her mind for a year now, refused to dwell on, forcibly removed from her consciousness, but a face that had always been there, slipping into her dreams at night, supposedly unwelcome but shamefully, gratefully received.

He had made her laugh.

The wedding she had dreaded had turned out to be the most exhilarating, heady night of her life, and it had all been down to Rico.

It had been Rico who had come up to her as she'd sat,

seemingly aloof but actually tense and awkward at the head table, watching confused and bewildered as Janey and Marco made a mockery of everything sacred and twirled around the dance floor.

Rico who had turned her world around.

'I need you to talk to me!' The urgency in his voice had caught Catherine completely off guard.

'Me?' Turning, she had opened her mouth, questions bobbing on her tongue as to why the most eligible of eligible bachelors should suddenly be paying attention to her. 'Why?' Catherine asked rudely.

'I'll tell you in a moment, but I really need for you to talk to me,' he insisted. 'I know this is probably the last thing you need right now, but I want you to look as if you're engrossed.'

She already was! It wasn't hard to give Rico Mancini her full attention, wasn't exactly a feat to stare into those dark, dark eyes and appear mesmerised. He had turned his chair so he was facing her. His knees casually apart he dragged her chair forward an inch or two, effectively caging her in, an earnest look on his face as he moved in closer and begged in low, urgent tones for her to stay put.

'What on earth's going on?' Catherine giggled, embarrassed and pleased and suddenly excited all at the same time.

'Would you believe me if I told you the minister's wife was coming on to me?'

'Esther?' Her mouth dropped open and her eyes automatically flicked across the room to gape in open disbelief at the paragon of virtue, dressed in twinset and pearls, her newly set hair lacquered firmly in place. She was scarcely able to believe Esther was capable of coming on to anyone. Mind you, Catherine mused as Esther's gaze wandered anxiously in their direction, from the effect two minutes up close with Rico was having on her, maybe even ministers' wives weren't immune.

'Don't look!' He put a hand up to her cheek, forcing her attention.

'I'm sorry.' Catherine was flustered, jumping a mile as he touched her, her cheeks stinging red as a blush worked its way upwards. She desperately tried to keep her voice even. 'Surely you've misread things!'

'That's what I told myself,' Rico agreed. 'That's what I kept on telling myself as she started fiddling with the buttons on my jacket....'

'She didn't!'

'That's not the half of it.' He gave a small shudder and Catherine started to laugh. 'If your sister had settled for a good Catholic wedding, then none of this would have happened.'

'That's Janey for you,' Catherine said dryly, and for a second so small it was barely there they shared a knowing smile.

'I excused myself, of course—said I had to get back to my girlfriend; so if you don't mind I'm going to have to borrow you for a while.'

'Borrow away.' Somehow she smiled. Somehow she accepted the champagne glass he offered with hands that were amazingly steady, given her heart-rate!

It had been the best night of her life—even if it had been a false togetherness; even if it had been just for Esther's benefit he'd made her feel special. Made her feel as if she was the only woman in the room.

Later, alone in his hotel room, those dark, brooding and

suspicious eyes had softened, gazing into hers as that strong, inscrutable face had moved in to kiss her. She could still almost taste the velvet of his lips, smell the heady tang of his cologne, feel her fingers in that jet hair as she had drowned in his kiss, responded to his urgent demands in a way she never had before. His kiss had fueled responses, unfamiliar, yet achingly welcome. Her breasts had pushed against his chest, her groin had pressed into his as his hand had worked the buttons of her dress, his frustration mounting as the tiny pink buttons proved too much for the frenzy of emotions that had gripped them. He'd ripped the pale pink tulle till her shoulders had been exposed, and she hadn't cared—hadn't cared he'd ruined her dress. She had hated it anyway, hated Janey for forcing her to wear it.

She had stood exposed but curiously excited, her dilated pupils struggling to focus, as one olive-skinned hand moved the fabric apart. The contrast of his dark skin on her soft white breast had caused her breath to catch in her throat, a tiny groan of ecstasy escaping as he'd buried his face in her bosom, his lips hot on her stinging nipples, flicking them with a firm tongue. The blood had rushed down—not to her breasts, though, down to her groin, and then the flicker of her first orgasm, as impatient hands slid up her legs, tearing the tiny panties aside. His fingers had snaked inside her wet warmth, his breath hot and hard as he sucked on her breasts, and she'd shuddered in the palm of his hand, lost in the frenzy of it all, stunned at how easily her body had responded, scarcely able to fathom how she could yield so much to him.

He had seemed to understand how overwhelmed she

had been, had held her afterwards, and for that slice of time, for one tiny moment, life had felt safe.

'We have to go back down,' he whispered into her hair as the world slowly drifted back into focus, seemingly understanding that this was alien for her, that she was feeling overwhelmed by the frenzy of emotion that had gripped her.

But even Rico's tender embrace wasn't enough to stop cruel reality invading, the sting of shame to prickle her senses. She barely knew this man, had met him only that night, and yet here she stood in his arms dishevelled, her groin still curiously alive, eyes glittering, cheeks flushed. Her arousal was still only a whisper away, yet he quelled her doubts in an instant, reading her mind as if she were a book.

'Don't regret this.' His voice was a low, delicious throb of reassurance in her ear. 'You are beautiful—this was beautiful.'

'I shouldn't have—'

'Hush.' His own arousal still pressed into her and she felt a stab of guilt: No longer the situation, but at her own selfishness, sure all the pleasure of the moment had been hers.

One woefully inexperienced hand tentatively moved down, clasping the steel of his erection, terrified of her own boldness, yet sure it was expected.

'Catherine, no.' His voice was breathless, his hand clamping over hers like a vice, and she flushed with embarrassment, terrified she had hurt him, sure he could feel the inexperience of her touch. 'We must go back, I am the best man and you are the bridesmaid. It is my brother's and your sister's wedding.'

'But I haven't…' She swallowed hard. 'You didn't…'

'There is time for that later.' His accent caressed her like a warm blanket on a cold night, and the glimpse of tomorrow, of another time, satisfied her craving in an instant. 'After the bride and groom leave I have to go to the airport, I have to go to the States, but before then we will talk—arrange to see each other again.' He kissed her then, slow and hard, but laced with tenderness.

She held onto his words all night, like a precious jewel clasped close to her chest, and it made the night bearable—made the night she had dreaded suddenly exciting.

'Well, you've changed your tune.'

Helping Janey out of her wedding dress and into her leaving outfit, Catherine was barely able to keep her hands still enough to undo the zipper.

Rico was downstairs waiting for her. In an hour or so she would be in his arms again.

'See—I knew if you actually let your hair down you might enjoy yourself.' Turning, Janey stared for a moment, taking in the dark, dishevelled curls, the glittering eyes and flushed cheeks. 'How come you changed your dress?' Her eyes dragged over the simple rust silk tunic Catherine had changed into, watching her sister's cheeks darken.

'Pink tulle really isn't my thing,' Catherine answered as blithely as she could with her heart in her mouth.

'Well, it's certainly Rico's thing. He couldn't take his eyes off you.' Calculating blue eyes narrowed thoughtfully. 'Where did you two disappear to after the speeches?'

'I don't know what you're talking about.' Catherine

was flustered, appalled that her sister might know. 'Come on, Janey, you'll miss your flight.'

'It will wait,' Janey said airily, 'When you've got your own private plane it doesn't leave without you.' Her voice dropped then, suddenly serious, and her eyes were wide with an urgency that made Catherine suddenly nervous. 'Play your cards right, sis, and all this could be yours.'

'Don't be ridiculous…'

'It really could. I've paved the way for you, Catherine, do you know how hard I had to work to convince Marco I wasn't just after him for his money? That I wasn't some cheap little gold-digger?'

'I don't want to talk about it, Janey.'

'But I *am* a cheap little gold-digger.' Janey gave a malicious smile. 'And now I'm married to a *very* rich man. You could do it too, Catherine.' She gave a dry, mirthless laugh as her sister shook her head and covered her ears, her voice rising in excitement as she pulled Catherine's hands away, enjoying her sister's embarrassment as she warmed to her subject. 'You hate your job, hate working with those awful children, hate your poky little flat…'

'Janey…' Catherine gave in then. Gave up trying to reason with her sister. Janey would never believe that even though she moaned about staff shortages and even her students at times, she loved her work—truly adored it. And, yes, her flat might be small, but it was home.

Tears were threatening now, at a vision of her sister so alive, so excited—such an appalling contrast to the cold, lifeless body that lay just a few rooms away. Balling her fists into her eyes, Catherine held them back. There was no point in tears, none at all. There was no one to wipe them—hadn't been since the day her parents had died—

and there was no one to comfort her tonight. Her memories flicked back in a second to the awful reality she faced—a reality she had to accept.

Janey was dead.

Rico despised her.

CHAPTER TWO

'CATHERINE.'

Gripping the jewellery tight in the palm of her hand, she stilled, her breath hot in her lungs. Even her heart seemed to stop for a second, then thudded back into action, tripping into a gallop as the scent that had fuelled her dreams for a year reached her nostrils, as the low drawl of one single word catapulted her senses into overdrive.

'Catherine?'

This time she looked up, praying somehow that the passage of time might render her impervious to his beauty, that a year might have dimmed the passion in those dark eyes, that somehow she might see that her imagination had been working overtime, had built him up to a status that cold reality would knock down. But if anything, Catherine realised, her imagination had underplayed his exquisiteness. Hadn't quite captured the haughty, effortless elegance, the razor-sharp cheekbones, the jet-dark hair, superbly cut, the tiny fan of silver at the temples that accentuated those inscrutable coal eyes.

'I came as soon as I heard.'

She didn't respond—*couldn't* respond. His presence was too overwhelming to allow for speech. Instead she gave a small nod, struggled with lips that didn't seem to know how to move any more.

'How long have you been here?'

'Since five.' Her voice was a croak, the two words all she could manage, but as his eyes bored into her Catherine realised more was called for and she cleared her throat, knowing he deserved the facts. It was his brother who was dead, after all. Their one night of passion and bitter parting had no place in this conversation, this was no time to rake over their past. 'I came back from work and the police were at my door. They drove me here.'

'Have they told you how it happened?' When she didn't answer he pushed harder. 'I know there was an accident. I know that Marco and Janey are both dead and that Lily is on the children's ward, but that is all I know.' His fists were bunched in tension. Catherine could see a muscle galloping in his taut cheek and she knew how hard it must be for a man like Rico, who always knew what was happening, always had everything in control, to be in the dark—to know that for once there was absolutely nothing he could do to put things right.

'I have tried to speak with the doctors and the police, but everyone who dealt with it directly is off duty. I will of course speak with them in the morning, but for now I would appreciate it if you could fill me in.'

His voice was supremely polite, as if he were addressing a stranger, and Catherine realised with a stab of sadness that that was exactly what she was to him—a stranger who had passed by once, no more and no less.

'Of course.' Again she cleared her throat, opened her mouth to speak, but his rather foreboding stance wasn't inspiring and she dragged her eyes away, resting her head in her hands and massaging her temples for a moment, willing eloquence to come.

'I need to know what happened, Catherine.' There was an impatient note to his voice.

'I'm trying to tell you, if you'd just—'

'I need to know *now*!' His fingers snapped in her face, an impatient Latin gesture that held no charm at all, and Catherine blinked and jumped back as Rico raised his voice. 'I am sorry you have had to deal with this—sorry you have had to face it all. But that is not my fault. I was in a closed meeting, my phone was off, and my secretary had taken an early flight back to Melbourne. I came as soon as I heard. I have been stuck in traffic, held up at the airport, and sitting on a plane going out of my mind with worry. I need some answers!'

The fire suddenly seemed to go out of him, his eyes taking in her shocked expression, the reddened rims of her eyes, the pale and trembling lips. 'I know it has been hard for you today, and I am sorry you have had to face this alone, but I am here now and I will take care of everything.'

'Take care of everything?' An incredulous laugh shot out of her pale lips, the anger that had simmered since the tragic news had been delivered, unleashed now. And however misdirected, however much this wasn't Rico's fault, he was the nearest target and Catherine turned a furious glare on him, her words coming out staccato, her body trembling with rage. How dare he waltz in here and demand answers? Swan in past midnight and say he would deal with it now when it had been she, Catherine, dealing with it—she alone facing the police, the social workers. She alone who had stood and identified the bodies.

'I have taken care of everything, Rico!' she shouted. 'Just as I took care of everything when my parents were killed. I should be used to it by now, I suppose. I guess I'm an old hand at identifying bodies and filling in forms!'

He didn't move a muscle, just stood in grim silence as her outburst continued, and his inaction incensed her, spurred her on to new levels of anger.

'I've been in this hospital for seven hours taking care of things, so don't you dare march in here and expect an eloquent detached statement, then snap your fingers in impatience if I don't speak quickly enough for you!' She looked up at him, her eyes furious and her chin jutting defiantly. 'I am not a member of your family, Rico, and neither am I one of your staff. You have no right to demand anything from me, no right at all. However, if you will sit down and exercise some patience I will tell you, as best I can, what little I know.'

For a second she thought he might hit her. Anger blazed in his eyes, the pent-up frustration of what must have been a hellish few hours undoubtedly exacerbated by her venom. But just as she thought she'd pushed him too far his wide shoulders slumped in an almost dejected fashion, and almost imperceptibly he gave a small nod, his Adam's apple bobbing a couple of times as he looked around the room, as if seeing it for the first time. Registering the fake leather chairs, he chose one next to her and sat down, raking a hand through his short hair, over the dark stubble of his chin, before turning to face her.

'I came as soon as I could,' he said again, but this time, his words were quiet, raw with emotion—apologetic even—his eyes utterly bereft as he stared at her, and for a tiny slice of time she caught a glimpse inside the beautiful head of Rico Mancini. Understood the pain behind the inscrutable mask he wore so effortlessly for she felt the agony of this senseless loss too.

'They went out for lunch,' Catherine started, her voice almost a whisper. 'They took Lily because apparently their nanny, Jessica, had walked out on them this morning.'

He opened his mouth, then closed it quickly, and Catherine gave a grateful nod. She would answer the whys in her own time.

'I went round last night, Rico.'

'You were there last night?' His eyes widened and she could almost hear his brain whirring into motion, almost foretell the questions on the tip of his tongue. But somehow he managed to hold them in, to let her tell her tale in her own time.

'I was at a parent-teacher night at school. It didn't finish till after nine, and for some reason—for some reason I...' Her fists clenched in her lap as the pain became almost more than she could bear, and only when he took her hand, only when he held it in his, was Catherine able to go on. 'I went round,' she whispered. 'I just couldn't be a bystander any more. What Janey and Marco got up to might have been their business, but if it was affecting Lily I couldn't just sit back and watch...'

Her eyes met his, imploring him to understand, and she was rewarded with a small nod. 'Of course they weren't at home, but I decided to wait. I spoke to Jessica—I wanted to find out if things were as bad as I feared or if I was just imagining it—and believe me she was only too happy to unload. Apparently she was sick of the way they carried on—the wild parties, the mess, and the fact they consistently *forgot* to pay her didn't help. It was supposed to have been her night off, but yet again Janey and Marco had gone out without telling her.'

Catherine was staring at their hands now, their fingers interlaced, and the contrast between them had never been more obvious. His dark and strong, a heavy watch on his wrist, such a contrast to her pale and trembling hands, an inkstain on her fingers, her nails short and neat but certainly not as groomed.

'We both waited for them to come home.'

For an age he said nothing, just held her hand tighter before gently saying, 'There was a confrontation?'

'I believe that would be the polite term for it.'

She screwed her eyes closed, the images of last night too horrible to relive. The harsh words she had spoken in anger were out now, with no hands of time to soothe them over the years.

'Jessica said she was leaving in the morning. That as soon as they'd sobered up enough to take responsibility for Lily she was going to get out of there—which is presumably why they took Lily to lunch with them,' Catherine carried on. 'You would have thought that might have slowed them down, forced them to behave responsibly...' Her voice trailed off, and this time when Rico broke in it wasn't unwelcome.

'They were drinking.' It wasn't a question, more a statement, but Catherine shook her head.

'I'm not sure what they were doing. According to the blood test Marco wasn't over the limit, but the police have ordered a drug screen. Apparently Marco was stumbling when they left the restaurant, and the doorman said he was utterly incoherent as they walked out. The *lunch* went till four. The only sensible thing they did all day was make sure that Lily was strapped in her car seat before they took off.'

'Who was driving?'

'Marco.'

'Was anyone else…?' His questions weren't rapid now, and they were no longer unwelcome. The whole sorry mess was easier shared.

'No one else was hurt. It seems Marco lost control or fell asleep at the wheel. They shot through the safety barrier onto the other side of the road, but thankfully they didn't hit anyone else.'

'Did they…?' Rico's eyes screwed closed and his fist balled again, only this time not in anger.

'Apparently they didn't suffer.' She repeated the nurse's words, hoping they might bring Rico the comfort that had eluded her, but the wry twist of his mouth told her the effect was about the same.

'They left that part to us.'

Us.

Even in the depths of despair the word offered a shelter for her mind to run to and hide for a while from the onslaught of the day and she took welcome refuge. Rico's hand tightened harder around hers; his grip warm and strong and it helped—helped her get through the next few seconds at least.

'Sorry to interrupt.' The nurse was back now, standing hesitantly at the door, a sympathetic smile on her young face and as Rico's hand dropped hers like a hot stone, cruel reality invaded.

There is no us, Catherine reminded herself. There never has been.

She was in this alone.

'I'm going off on my break in a few minutes. Would you like me to walk you back up to the children's ward before I go? It's a bit of a maze...'

'That won't be necessary, thank you.' Rico stood up, the tenderness she had briefly witnessed flicking off like a light switch, as he asserted his authority in an instant. 'I have already been to the children's ward and seen Lily. I explained to the sister in charge that Miss Masters and I will be staying at a nearby hotel tonight and will be back first thing in the morning. Thank you,' he said again crisply, effectively dismissing her, and as the door closed Catherine blinked at him a couple of times.

'You've been to see Lily?'

'Of course.'

Of course. The words played over in her mind. Of course he would have been to see her first. Marco and Janey were dead, there was nothing he could do there, why wouldn't he rush to see his niece? It made perfect sense, but a chill of foreboding crept over her as she met his dark, brooding stare, saw his eyes narrow suspiciously as he watched her.

'I don't want to go to a hotel and leave her.' Catherine stood up, relieved that her legs, although still trembling, seemed at least to be holding her now. 'I don't think she should be alone tonight. If she wakes up—'

'The nurses will deal with her,' Rico said crisply 'And if there is a problem we are only two minutes away. That is why I have booked into a hotel rather than go home; we will be literally across the road.'

'But I'd be next to her here,' Catherine pointed out. 'Just because you're too grand to sleep on a roller bed it doesn't mean that I am.'

'I make no apology,' Rico clipped. 'I would like to shower, I would like a very large drink, and...' Whatever else he wanted, Rico wasn't sharing it. He stared haughtily back at her. 'I'm sure the nurses will be able to cope with her.'

'But she needs—'

'What?' Rico broke in, his word a pistol shot. 'Needs what? You can't miss what you don't have, and I doubt that baby has ever seen her mother after six p.m. In the six months Lily's been alive she's already had to get to know five nannies, so I'm sure a nurse feeding her in the middle of the night isn't going to send her into a frenzy. Your sister made quite sure Lily got used to strangers.'

Your sister. He had spat the words at her accusingly but Catherine refused to rise.

'I want to be with her,' Catherine stated calmly. 'If you want to go to a hotel—fine. But I'm not leaving.' Picking up her bag, she headed for the door, but the slow hand-clap resounding from Rico stilled her. Tossing her head, she turned to face him, her eyes questioning.

'Bravo,' he sneered. 'If I didn't know you better you'd almost pass for a grief-stricken aunty.'

'I just want to do the right thing by Lily,' Catherine responded, utterly bemused, with no idea where this was leading.

'Of course you do!' She heard the sarcasm dripping in his voice, but it merely confused her. 'Possession is nine-tenths of the law and all that.'

'I don't know what you're talking about.' Whatever Rico's problem was she didn't want to hear it. She didn't want to do this now. She was exhausted, physically and mentally exhausted, and even though she'd only been promised a roller bed by Lily's cot the thought of stretching out, of closing her eyes on this vile day, was the only thing keeping her standing. 'I'll speak to you in the morning.'

'You'll speak to me tonight.' His voice stayed low but there was a menacing note that had the hairs rising on the back of her neck. 'You'll tell me everything that's happened.'

'I've already told you,' Catherine responded hotly. 'What the hell does it matter how it happened, Rico? They're dead, and going over and over it doesn't change anything.'

'Oh, but it does.' His eyes bored into hers. 'The fact they're dead changes everything. Why didn't you tell me you'd spoken to social workers, Catherine? Why did you omit to mention that you've told them you are taking Lily home with you when she's discharged? That you are applying for guardianship?'

Her mind was working nineteen to the dozen now, realisation dawning as his savage eyes met hers, as she registered just how low he thought she was prepared to stoop.

'You've got it all wrong,' she insisted. 'It wasn't like that. The hospital needed a name, a next of kin, someone to sign a consent form if Lily needed an operation.'

'And you were only too happy to provide it.'

'Of course I was,' Catherine responded hotly. 'As much as you mightn't like it, Rico, as much as you might want to wipe me out of your life, I have as much right to be here as you. I am Lily's aunt just as you are her uncle, and given the fact that her parents have just been killed it makes us her next of kin. I had every right to sign that form and I resent the implication that I had some sort of ulterior motive. She's seems okay now, but we didn't know. She has bruises from the car seat and the doctors thought there could be some internal damage. You weren't here, Rico! What was I supposed to do? Refuse to sign?'

'Okay,' he conceded reluctantly. 'But you told them you are taking Lily home with you when she's discharged, told them you are prepared to look after her...'

'And I am,' Catherine wailed, her patience flying out of the window as she faced this impossible, mistrusting man. 'She's my niece and I want to look after her—in the short term at least.'

'That's not what you said to the social workers.'

'Oh, come on, Rico. Janey died this afternoon. I can barely comprehend what's happened, let alone make long-term plans! As if I know what I'm going to do.'

'Don't lie,' he spat. '*Poor little Lily*. I can just see you laying it on with a trowel to the social workers. I can almost hear the little sob in your voice as you said it!' His eyes narrowed, his lips contorting as he eyed her distastefully. 'Only she's not so poor, is she? As of this evening, Lily's incredibly rich. You must have been rubbing your hands in glee when the bloody Mancinis couldn't even be bothered to make it to the hospital—rubbing your hands in glee when no one was there to stop you when you said you'd take care of her.'

'It wasn't like that!' It was Catherine's voice rising now. 'How dare you? How dare you accuse me of trying to profit from my sister's death? How dare you suggest I would use my niece as a pawn? Why would I—'

'I'll tell you why.' His voice was low, a contrast to hers, his eyes forbidding as they stared back at her coldly. 'Because you hate your life, Catherine. Because you'd go to any lengths to change it.'

'You're disgusting.' Pulling her arms away, she attempted to wrestle it from his hand, but his grip only tightened. 'Let go of me, Rico. I'm going to my niece.'

'Over my dead body.' His face was as white as marble in the fluorescent light, his cheeks jagged, his lips set in grim determination. 'You're coming back to the hotel with me, Catherine. Tonight we talk.'

CHAPTER THREE

THEY drove in silence.

Angry denials were bobbing on her tongue, but the set of his jaw, the grip of his hands on the steering wheel told her now wasn't the time.

They needed to face the situation calmly, talk things through rationally. Lily's future was too precious to be relegated to a heated row in a hospital corridor, and given the day's events a high-speed sports car wasn't exactly the ideal spot either. That was the only reason Catherine had given in and agreed to go back to the hotel, allowed him to lead her through the endless hospital corridors and out to the car park, and she held her tongue now, biting back smart replies, determined to do things properly.

His sleek, low silver car purred through the night streets. The windows thankfully were open, and Catherine welcomed the cool breeze that whipped her cheeks, blowing away the nauseating stench of the hospital. As they slowed at the lights a tram clattered past. A couple of young lovers were kissing in a doorway, and the early editions of tomorrow's papers were already bundled outside a newsagents'. It was hard to comprehend that the world was carrying on as normal, hard to fathom that those same newspapers probably contained a line or two, maybe even a photo, summarising the tragic end of Janey and Marco for those who wanted to know.

The concierge greeted Rico as if he had been waiting

up only for him to arrive, making impatient gestures in
Reception to hurry things along.

'Mr Mancini, this is such an unexpected pleasure. I was
just saying that we haven't seen you or...' His warm
greeting was barely acknowledged and even in her numb
state Catherine felt a sting of embarrassment at Rico's
cool treatment of the staff.

'I would like to go straight up, please.'

'Your bags are already on their way up, and the housekeeper is turning back the bed as we speak. It will be just
a moment—'

'I don't have a moment.' Rico's voice was pure, un-
adulterated snobbery. 'Miss Masters is tired, I am tired,
and I'm going to my room!' Striding to the lift, he beckoned a furiously blushing Catherine to join him, punching
the top button and closing the door on the poor concierge.

'You really think you're better than everyone, don't
you?'

For once Rico didn't respond, for once a smart reply
seemed to elude him, and Catherine warmed to her subject
as the lift door slid open on the heady heights of the
penthouse. She watched as he dismissed the frenziedly
working staff with one flick of his hand and let out a low
snort, shaking her head as he poured himself a drink, not
even bothering to offer her one.

'You haven't even booked a room here, yet you expect
one to be waiting for you—for people to jump just because you deign to grace them with your presence.'

'What do you expect me to do, Catherine?' He downed
his drink in one, slamming the crystal onto the silver tray,
his eyes finally meeting hers. 'Tell me how you expected
me to behave down there.'

'You could have shown some manners, to start with,' Catherine replied hotly, and even though the argument was meaningless, even though it was so far removed from all that had happened, she prolonged it. Maybe it was easier than facing the real reason why she was here. 'The concierge was being nothing but pleasant—'

'He's paid to be pleasant,' Rico broke in. 'He's paid to remember my name, to remember that this is where my brother and I come for lunch when my schedule allows, that sometimes I choose to stay here rather than drive home.'

'Maybe he is paid to remember, but surely you can still be polite when someone greets you!'

'My brother is dead,' Rico snapped.

'So is my sister. But I don't use it as an excuse to snub people. I didn't treat the nurses and doctors like dirt on my shoe...'

'If I hadn't interrupted him he would have asked about Marco, asked how he was doing, when they could expect to see him again. Did you want me to tell him, Catherine? Did you want me to stand in the foyer and tell the world my brother is dead when any moment now they're going to find out anyway?'

He looked at her bemused face and shook his head disbelievingly. Picking up a remote control, he flicked on the television, watching her expression as the images shot into focus, hearing the tiny strangled sob as the mangled wreckage of a car filled the screen, then Marco and Janey's wedding photo, superimposed on the top right corner. The news reader droned on, regaling supposed facts Catherine simply wasn't ready to hear, and her hand shot to her ears in a childlike gesture, her eyes screwing

closed against the horrible images that seemed to be chok-
ing her.

'I asked the hospital not to release their names until we
left.'

His explanation wasn't helping, and she opened her
eyes, stared at him, bemused.

'A Mancini is dead.'

'Two Mancinis,' Catherine corrected. 'My sister counts
too.'

'Your sister counts for nothing,' Rico sneered. 'But,
yes, I stand corrected. Technically two Mancinis are dead,
Catherine, and that is news. No doubt the *poor concierge*
you were so worried about is now either kicking himself
for his insensitivity or ringing the press to tell them I am
here.' He gave a small shrug. 'Frankly, I don't give a
damn which one it is.'

'But why would the press want to speak to you?'

'Are you stupid, Catherine? Or just a really good actress?'

His words barely touched the sides. Pain was already
layered on top of pain—another dash of scorn, another
dose of humiliation from Rico was not much in the
scheme of things.

'I'm not stupid, Rico.' Her brown eyes met his. 'I read
the papers, I watch the news when I get home from work,
and I know how powerful the Mancinis are, I know that
the stockmarket rises and falls depending on your company's profits. But Marco wasn't a part of the family business—Marco never worked a day in his life. I really can't
see why the press are getting so excited. His death isn't
going to affect the company—'

'Do you think the press will care about a small detail like that?' Rico broke in, 'Marco is rich, he has a daughter—'

'*Was* rich,' Catherine corrected, and for a second so small it was barely there she was sure she saw a flicker of pain in those dark eyes, saw the haughty, bland mask slip for a tiny second, but she continued anyway. '*Had* a daughter.'

'Which is why I've brought you here.'

'You didn't bring me here,' Catherine pointed out. 'I chose to come. I'm not stupid, Rico, but possibly I've been a bit naïve. Maybe the world isn't going to stop because of Janey and Marco's deaths, but it's certainly going to pause for a few days' reflection, and I can see that Lily's future will be debated vigorously by people who don't give a damn about her. But I for one don't care what the newspapers have to say, because at the end of the day everyone will get on with their lives. We're the ones who are going to be living it; we're the ones dealing with the issues.'

'I don't give a damn what the press say, either,' Rico responded. 'But it is not only the press who will be having their say…' His eyes narrowed thoughtfully and he stared at her for the longest moment, as if deciding whether or not to continue. 'My stepmother is not going to let you have Lily.' A tiny gasp of protest escaped Catherine's lips, but she swallowed it back. Rico's words were too important for interruption. 'I can tell you now that she won't allow it to happen. She will not allow Lily's inheritance to leave the family.'

'But why?' Catherine asked, bemused. 'Surely she doesn't need the money? Surely…?'

'Too much is never enough, and the way my step-

mother spends money this unexpected windfall will not
be given up without a fight.' His mouth set in a grim line.
'My stepmother is the coldest woman on this earth. She
is the reason Marco went off the rails, the reason he drank
himself—'

'That's an excuse,' Catherine broke in. 'I had the same
argument over and over with Janey, when she tried to
blame our parents for whatever scrape she found herself
in. You had the same family as Marco, the same pressures,
yet you still managed to hold down a job, manage your
affairs. Marco may have been disadvantaged by his stepmother, but he still had a lot more opportunities in life
than most people dream of. You do him no favours by
blaming your stepmother.'

'Perhaps,' Rico conceded. 'But it is not always black
and white, Catherine. People are different. I am stronger
than Marco; I am tougher.' There was no superiority in
his words, just the cool deliverance of fact, and this time
Catherine chose not to remind him that Marco was now
in the past tense. She just listened as he continued to talk.
'Antonia is a nasty piece of work, and till the day I die I
will blame her in part for the fact Marco is now lying in
a mortuary...' His voice wavered slightly, his fists clenching in salute by his sides, and Catherine was shocked to
see what was surely the glint of tears in those dark eyes.
But just as soon as his pain registered, like a light flicking
off, the impassive mask returned. 'I will not allow her to
mess up Lily the way she messed up Marco.'

'Then what was all that about back at the hospital?'
Deliberately she kept her tone even, refusing to be intim-
idated by him. 'Given what you've just told me, surely
I'm the better option to raise Lily? And before you insist

I only want her for the money, let me tell you, Rico, you are wrong. Her inheritance never entered my head—not until you came tonight.'

He stared at her, disbelief etched on his features, but his shrug was almost weary. 'Maybe you want both. Maybe you do care for Lily, and I guess there is no shame in wanting to be rich.' She opened her mouth to argue, but Rico carried on talking. 'I cannot let Lily go with this woman, Catherine.'

'Then let me have her.'

'It is not that simple. Antonia will go to every court in the land, use every means available to discredit you. She'll have the most expensive lawyers. You are a teacher, Catherine. The reality is that you survive on a schoolteacher's wage. Against her you won't stand a chance.'

His words made sense, and a dark feeling of foreboding shivered through her. Though it galled her to ask for his assistance, Catherine knew she had no choice, and the words were out before the idea had even formed. 'You could help me.'

'Why would I help you, Catherine? Why wouldn't I just apply for custody myself?'

'Go ahead,' Catherine said airily, though her heart was in her mouth. She registered the surprise in his expression and it gave her a small surge of triumph. Her eyes met his defiantly, fighting fire with fire as she carried on talking. 'But don't try and scare me off, Rico, with talk of money and lawyers. I'll sell my home if I have to, and when the money has gone I'll apply for legal aid. I'll tell you this now, and I'll tell each Mancini in turn if they care to ask: I have as much right to Lily as anyone. Unlike you, I've actually played a part in her short life. As much as I loathed the way Marco and Janey carried on I still went round, still made sure I was there for Lily…'

'I've been busy with work,' Rico argued. 'And watching those two made me—'

'Save it,' Catherine snapped. 'Tell the court how you couldn't even get away for her christening, how you saw your niece for two minutes at the hospital the day after she was born and that you haven't seen her since.'

'There are reasons!' Rico roared, but Catherine just glared back.

'Excuses,' Catherine flared. 'They are nothing but excuses! And now you have the gall to tell me you want custody of Lily—a baby you've barely met. Well, I'm not going to let you do it, Rico. I don't give a damn about the Mancini fortune, and your power doesn't frighten me. I will fight for her, and deep down I think you know that I'm the best person for her.'

'*You?*'

She heard the scorn and contempt in his voice and deliberately kept hers even. 'Yes, me, Rico. I will fight for Lily. I will do whatever it takes to ensure her future. Whatever it takes,' Catherine repeated, just to be sure he understood. 'I know you don't think much of me, Rico. You made that abundantly clear on the night of the wedding '

'That night has no bearing on this discussion.'

'Oh, but it does.' The sting of embarrassment brought a flush of colour to her pale cheeks, but Catherine refused to be silenced. Lily's future was too important for her to dodge behind embarrassing facts. 'You were the one who treated me like a cheap tart, Rico.' She saw him wince at her brutal words, but ploughed on anyway. 'You were the one who walked out of the reception without even a good-bye…' Her cheeks were red now, but not with embarrassment. Instead it was with a year's worth of humiliation and anger at this man who had treated her with such contempt. 'I ran after you, Rico. I came to your car and knocked on your window and you refused to even look at me…'

'Because you disgusted me.'

Her recoil was so visible he might as well have hit her. The colour that had suffused her cheeks drained, and tears that had stayed buried all day, were stinging now, but Catherine bit them back, refusing to let him see her cry, to allow him the glory of her utter humiliation.

'Might I remind you, Rico—' her voice was strained but dignified, her lips barely moving as she struggled to hold it together '—that it takes two? And if you're going to try and use that night to discredit me in court then it won't work. You were very much a participant in what happened.'

'What are you talking about?' he sneered.

'Presumably you're one of those chauvinist men who assume it's okay for men to behave in such a fashion but that's it somehow different for women?' He opened his mouth to speak but Catherine overrode him, her voice coming louder now. 'And maybe you're right, Rico. Because try as I might I cannot justify what happened that night. I cannot explain to anyone, let alone myself, how I ended up in a hotel room with a man I barely knew. Yes, I behaved like a cheap tart—so you see, Rico, you can't hurt me with your cruel words, can't shame me any more than I shamed myself that night. I may disgust you, but I can assure you I disgust myself more.'

They stood in bristling silence, her words resonating like an awful echo until Catherine could no longer bear it—couldn't bear to stand there a moment longer. Her eyes scanned the luxurious room for an exit, settling instead for the safety of the bathroom, and only when she'd closed the door did she let out the breath she had been inadvertently holding. Her jaw was aching from gritting her teeth together.

How could she explain to him that to her dying day she would never be able to fathom how she had so brazenly allowed him to touch her, hold her? That even a year on she could scarcely comprehend the intimacies she had shared with a virtual stranger that night? But he hadn't seemed like a stranger, Catherine recalled, resting her burning face against the mirror as she remembered the passion that had gripped her, that had sullied her sensibility and overridden her normal reservation.

How could she explain to Rico what she couldn't understand herself?

Peeling off her clothes, Catherine stepped into the shower, the welcome bliss of water on her body soothing somehow, giving her a few moments to compose herself, to sort through the jumble of events today had thrown at her. She wished she could stay there for ever, wished she could hide from the world for just a moment longer, but somehow she had to be strong, had to go back in that room and face him.

For Lily's sake.

Pulling on a thick white robe, she tied it firmly before filling the sink to wash her stockings and knickers. Luxurious as the hotel might be, it didn't come with a fully stocked wardrobe—and anyway she was glad of the chance to prolong the discussion a few moments longer.

'What are you doing?'

Appalled, she swung round, scarcely able to believe his gall.

'How dare you come in here without knocking?' Eyes blazing, she met his gaze. 'How dare you come in here? I could have been naked...'

'You are dressed in a robe,' Rico pointed out, clearly unmoved at her protests. 'We need to talk, and instead you are hiding in here.'

'I'm not hiding,' Catherine lied, but Rico just shook his head.

'Why are you washing your clothes like some gipsy in the river, then?' he sneered. 'You *are* hiding, Catherine...'

'You really are the limit—do you know that? For your information, I didn't stop to pack an overnight bag when the police arrived at my door.'

'Send your washing down to Housekeeping, then.' Rico shrugged.

'I have some pride,' Catherine retorted. 'Not much, I admit that—you've managed to obliterate most of it—but if you think I'm going to hand my underwear over to be washed and ironed then you've got another think coming.' Very deliberately she turned away, rinsing out her washing and draping it over the bath ledge, making sure she took her time, sensing his bristling impatience yet refusing to be rushed, refusing to turn as he commenced the discussion she had hoped to delay.

'If Lily were older undoubtedly we could ask her what

she wanted. But given she is only six months old, that is of course impossible.'

She could feel his eyes on her, but she didn't turn, just gave a small nod as Rico continued.

'So perhaps we should ask ourselves what her parents would have wanted?'

His words made sense, and reluctantly she turned to face him, willing to at least listen to what Rico had to say.

'Marco and I may have rowed on occasion, and I may have alienated myself from him to some degree because I didn't approve of his lifestyle, but we still met up regularly. As I said before, we came to this hotel for many lunches, and whatever trouble he was in Marco knew he could always call on me. I know that he did respect me.' His voice thickened and he swallowed hard before continuing. 'I know in my heart that he loved me, Catherine, and I also know he would have wanted me to raise his child. So now it's your turn. What about Janey?'

His eyes never left her face, taking in every flicker of reaction as his question reached her. 'What would Janey have wanted for Lily?'

'She'd have wanted me to have her…' Her voice trailed off, her startled eyes blinking rapidly, and Rico leapt in, sensing weakness and exploiting it in an instant.

'Because she loved you?' His voice was so silken you might almost have missed the derisive sneer, but Catherine was like a radar where Rico was concerned, and she flinched at his insensitivity. 'Janey would have wanted you to have Lily because she adored her big sister Catherine?'

'She did love me; I was her sister.' Her lips were impossibly dry and she ran her tongue over them, her head spinning as he relentlessly continued.

'You don't have to love your sister, Catherine,' Rico pointed out mercilessly. 'You don't even have to love your husband—and Janey didn't love Marco, did she? *Did she?*' He roared the words the second time—the roar of a lion defending its territory, of a beautiful animal to be admired from a distance, but that could turn in a second. 'In fact Marco was just a walking, talking chequebook to his young bride…'

'Rico, please…' Catherine started. She wanted him to stop, wanted to end this horrible interrogation, didn't want to sully the few precious memories she had with the awful truth—didn't want to admit even to herself how little Janey had thought of her.

'Janey wanted the fast cars, the nice home, the maids, the lifestyle—and I don't doubt she'd have wanted the same for her daughter.'

'Janey would have wanted me,' Catherine insisted, but the lack of conviction in her voice truly terrified her. 'You've got it all wrong, Rico.'

'Have I?' His eyes narrowed thoughtfully. 'Which part?'

'All of it,' Catherine whispered, pleating the tie of her robe with trembling fingers. And she knew there and then that she could never admit to the truth. Rico was right, damn him, and it hurt to admit it. Janey hadn't loved her; Janey had hated her. More damaging than that, Janey had blatantly admitted she had married Marco for his money. If it ever got out, if Catherine ever admitted the truth, what chance would she have against the family courts?

What chance would she have against the might of Rico Mancini? It would all be over bar the shouting.

Lily would be gone from her life as surely as she was standing here now.

A lion Rico might be, but the lioness in Catherine emerged then— proud and wary, sleek and refined, and willing to do whatever it took to protect those she loved. To her dying breath she would deny it. She would take Janey's words to the grave. Would lie through her teeth if that was what it took.

Lily needed her.

'Janey loved Marco.'

'She told you that?'

Dragging in air through her clenched teeth, she wrenched her eyes from the floor and forced herself to do the hardest thing she had done in her life—look Rico in the eye and lie.

'Yes, Rico. She told me that she loved him. Janey loved Marco and his money had nothing to do with it. I know in my heart that—'

'Save it.' A well-manicured hand flicked in the air. His eyes were more shuttered than ever, his voice almost weary, and for once there was economy in his actions, the usual extravagant Latin temperament curiously subdued as he halted her speech. 'It is time for bed.'

'I thought we were going to talk,' Catherine protested, following him out of the bathroom, confused at the sudden change in his demeanour. She had braced herself for confrontation, adrenaline pumping through her veins as she geared up to defend herself, to do whatever it took to keep Lily near. But all the fight seemed to have left Rico now. Suddenly all he looked was exhausted. 'I thought we were going to talk, Rico,' she said again. 'That is why I came here after all; we need to sort something out.'

'And we will,' Rico affirmed. 'But I realise now is not the time. We cannot decide anything tonight; we are both tired and it has been an emotional day.'

She almost laughed—almost laughed at his detached summing up. The man who stood before her seemed curiously void of emotion.

'Here.' He handed her a crisp white shirt. 'I always have a spare in my briefcase. You can sleep in this.'

'Rico?' Even as the word was out Catherine knew she would get no response. His apathy unnerved her and, though she was loath to admit it, somehow she preferred the angry, volatile man she was starting to get used to.

'It is time to sleep, Catherine. You can have the master bedroom; I'll take the other.'

It should have been uncomfortable, awkward—in any other circumstances sharing a suite with the man who had so carelessly broken her heart would have sent Catherine into a spin. But not tonight.

Tonight was for Janey.

By the time she had popped back into the bathroom and pulled on the shirt Rico had left the lounge, and she stood for an uncertain moment before heading to the open door of his room; he was already stretched out on his bed, his hands behind his head, staring fixedly at the ceiling. Catherine knew his averted gaze had nothing to do with the heated words they had shared, or the problems they faced. Knew that his pensive shift in tempo had grief written all over it.

'Goodnight, then.' She hovered by his door, awaiting a

response that never came, before gently closing the door and heading for her own room.

As the light flicked off and darkness descended the oblivion she so desperately craved didn't come, but the horrors of the day did recede slightly as she drifted to the gentle past...

Suddenly she was away from the sullied world Janey had created, back to two little girls, one dark, one blonde. The Janey she chose to remember danced in her mind— Janey before their parents' death, Janey before money and greed had taken over. The little sister she had grown up with was ready to be mourned now, and Catherine drifted back to the beauty of a past when the world had seemed good and safe. Suddenly she was scared to go there, scared of the depth of her pain, scared to take the lid off her grief, terrified of what she might find. The past a mocking reminder of the void left today.

An involuntary sob escaped her lips and she bit it back hard, gulping into the darkness, her breath coming in short, ragged bursts as she struggled to hold it in—hold in eight years of agony, eight years of pain, eight years of being alone and having to be the strong one.

She had learnt long ago the folly of tears, the loneliness of weeping into the night with no one to wipe them away.

And she would *not* cry now.

'Catherine?'

She heard the concern in his voice but she didn't answer, just lay frozen in the darkness, her ears on elastic as he crossed the room, feeling the indentation of the mattress as he lowered himself onto the bed.

'Catherine, are you okay?'

She nodded, her hand shielding her eyes as he flicked on the light.

'You are allowed to cry, you know,' Rico offered gently, but she shook her head.

'Crying won't bring them all back.'

'All?' When she didn't answer he carried on gently. 'You're not just talking about Janey and Marco, are you, Catherine?'

She didn't respond, but he pushed on gently. 'What happened to your parents?'

'They died,' she said simply.

'Tell me about it.'

She was about to say no, to shake her head and turn away, but something stopped her. A need to share, to delve a little into her past—a past she simply couldn't face alone tonight. And even if Rico despised her, even if this conversation would be forgotten, or even held against her in the cold light of day, tonight the simple fact that it was another human being, reaching out in the lonely abyss of grief, was enough to make her open up.

'My mother was beautiful.' Catherine's voice quivered, and she cleared her throat before going on. 'Her name was Lily as well, and my father would have done anything for her.'

'Like Janey and Marco?'

'In some ways,' Catherine admitted. 'Although my father was always very sensible where the children were concerned. Just not with my mother.' She gave a wry laugh, but it held no malice. 'My mother decided she wanted to go skiing, just like that. She saw an advert on the television and demanded my father take her to the snow. It didn't matter to her that it was a five-hour drive, didn't matter to her that my father had never even seen snow, let alone driven in it, or that they didn't have chains for the car; she wanted to go and that was all there was to it.'

Rico's hand moved across the bed, capturing hers as she screwed her eyes tightly closed, and somehow his touch gave her the strength to continue, to tell her sorry tale.

'Needless to say they never made it. The police turned up at my home just as they did today, said just what the nurse did this afternoon—''They wouldn't have suffered.'''

'But you did.' His free hand moved to her face, brushing away a heavy dark curl then lingering there, tracing the apple of her cheek, the high arch of eyebrow, before capturing her face in his hand. She ached to turn to him, his touch a comfort she craved, but still she lay there frozen. 'What happened then?'

'Their affairs were a mess.' Catherine closed her eyes for a second, the tension and the agony of those times still painful even now. 'I took a couple of jobs to support Janey and I...'

'You still went to college, though?'

Catherine nodded. 'Maybe I shouldn't have. Maybe I should have been there more for Janey. I just thought if I could get my training over, forge a decent career, then eventually we'd both be okay. Clearly I was wrong.'

'Janey chose how to live her life,' Rico suggested gently, but Catherine refused to be comforted.

'Eventually I sold the house.' Her lip quivered slightly. 'I just couldn't handle the mortgage repayments. I put a deposit on a flat with my half; I hoped Janey would do the same with hers. She didn't,' Catherine added need-lessly. 'Instead she blew the money on fancy clothes and restaurants, renting apartments she could never afford. No matter how I tried to reel her in, no matter how I tried to slow her spending down, she spun out of control.'

Tears were precariously close now, but still she bit them back, clenched her eyes closed, raked in some air in an effort to hold on. When she opened them Rico was still there, his eyes not mocking now, infinitely patient as he sat there.

'You have lost so much, Catherine; there is no shame in tears.'

'There's no point either.' She gave a tired shrug. 'I learnt that eight years ago, Rico. Tears don't change anything.'

'I don't agree,' Rico murmured. 'Sometimes it is better to feel pain than to feel nothing.'

And Catherine wished perhaps more than she had ever wished for anything that she could do it. Could let out some of what she held in. But as the silence lingered on, as her tears stayed firmly away, it was Rico who broke the loaded silence, Rico who summed it all up in four simple words.

'I will miss him.'

Still she didn't respond, just lay there staring as Rico softly continued. 'It hurts when I think of Marco. It is agony to know that he is never coming back...' His hand was still on her face, and as he spoke this time she did turn her cheek, nestle a little in the warmth of his touch. 'Marco was born in this country.' Rico smiled gently. 'I used to look after him. I didn't want him to go through what I went through.'

When Catherine's eyes narrowed, Rico's smile widened a touch. 'When I started school I spoke no English. I was the little Sicilian boy with the lunch that smelt. Salami and forty-degree heat is not a good mix. And I suppose Marco looked up to me for a while, came to me if he was in trouble.' There was a wistful note to his voice, then a tiny swallow before he continued. 'I only wish he had carried on looking up to me; carried on coming to me for advice instead of going off the rails. But even though I knew he did stupid things, knew he made mistakes, still I loved him. He wasn't always bad.'

'Nor was Jancy.' She saw his shoulders stiffen, a denial undoubtedly bobbing on his tongue, but instead he nodded, afforded her the right to remember her sister as she saw fit.

He sat just a breath away, his presence no longer intimidating, but strangely comforting. The lamplight drew dark shadows on his torso, highlighting the magnificence of his shoulders, defining the quiet strength of his muscular body, imparting confidence. A weary five o'clock shadow dusted his jaw now, but there was veracity in each and every tear that glittered in those brooding eyes—not mocking now, not clouded with suspicion, just infinitely understanding, giving the acquiescence she needed to continue.

'I was thinking about when we were little—how we used to play, how she used to make me laugh. She was always the naughty one...' a sob caught in her throat, 'I can't believe she's really gone.'

He pulled her towards him then, scooping her in his arms and wrapping them around her, a shield, a rock to cling to. 'Let it out, Catherine. Now is not the time to hold back.'

Oh, how she wanted to. How badly she wanted to give way to the tears that were threatening. This glimpse of his tenderness was taking her back to their first night together, when emotion had won, when feelings had been followed, and she was grateful to him—grateful to Rico for crossing the room, for taking her in his arms and telling her that he hurt too, for allowing her to glimpse that behind the cool façade beat a mortal heart that hurt too sometimes, that got broken, that mourned.

But she couldn't quite go there. Couldn't give in to the tears that threatened to drown her. So instead she held him, held him ever closer. There was something about grief that suspended morals, something about loneliness that broke all the rules—because she didn't want to be alone tonight and knew that neither did he. She didn't want the light to go off, to be plunged back into the hell of the twilight zone she had inhabited moments before, and as he held her, caressed her, she was aware, achingly aware, of the shift in tempo. His caress was not so much comforting now, but urgent. His body beneath her fingers was now not so safe and reassuring. There was a tingling awareness of his skin against hers, his lips tracing her cheeks, and it was far easier to drown in his kiss than to face a night alone. Far easier to seek solace in the escape his touch afforded than face cruel reality…

Oh, she might regret it, might see the folly of her ways later, but she craved oblivion now—craved the balmy bliss only Rico could provide. And as his tongue slid inside her parted lips, as his hand cupped her breast through the crisp cotton, she knew Rico craved it too.

Her body arched towards his, long legs coiling around his hips, and he impatiently pulled at the shirt, kicked off his boxers until she could feel his manhood against her, swollen and urgent against her thighs. His lips were hot and urgent over her stomach as she lifted her arms, allowing him to slide the shirt away, and then he pushed her gently down, parted her legs with his hands.

She stared, mesmerized, as he knelt before her, a knot of fear, excitement, anticipation welling as she eyed the velvet steel of his erection. Its sight was more intoxicating than any drink, blurring her senses into one, transfixed on this moment. Her pulse fluttered in a throat that seemed to constrict and she dragged her eyes to his, her whole body on high alert as he lifted the peach of her buttocks slightly from the sheets, held her aching and impatient in his hands and guided her towards him. A stab of pain so delicious she cried out for a moment. Her legs were coiling around him, dragging him deeper, moving against him.

Hot breath burned on her shoulders as he moved inside her, his muscles taut beneath her touch, and she surrendered herself utterly. Focusing only on him—his skin, his smell, the salty, heady taste of him. She could hear her own gasps growing louder, could feel the rise and fall of her breasts as they moulded into him. The flush of her orgasm was whooshing up her cheeks, a dizzy, heady glow, and her thighs trembled convulsively. She could feel him growing more inside her, his breathing uneven, a low groan building inside as he bucked against her, his buttocks taut as she dragged her nails over him, in an animal frenzy as they climaxed together, contracting with an intensity more than merely physical. She could hear him call her name, but it seemed to be from a distance. She called his too, searching for him in the darkness, both calling out as they found the emotional haven they craved, and for a second she knew he needed her—that this release was as necessary as it was wondrous.

And after, as he held her, as he reached over and turned out the light, she no longer feared the darkness. For no dark imaginings could hurt her with Rico by her side.

CHAPTER FOUR

FOR a moment it was all okay.

For one stolen moment between awakening and opening her eyes the world seemed right, but a strange sensation gripped her, a horrible sense of foreboding, and Catherine mentally tried to fathom what was wrong. The truth dawned with a sickening thud as her eyes snapped open.

Jancy was dead.

'Here.' A cup of coffee was placed on the bedside table and, pulling the sheet around her, Catherine sat up, taking a grateful sip of the liquid as she tried to fathom all that had happened. She'd never had a hangover, but from Janey's description this must come precariously close, and she eyed the dripping percolator, already planning her second cup. She could see the crumpled shirt lying on the floor, Rico's dark boxers beside it—evidence if ever it was needed of what had taken place. Under any other circumstances it would have overwhelmed her, but not today. Her grief was too overwhelming to allow much else.

'My father just called. He and Antonia are at the airport; they'll be here tomorrow.'

Catherine looked up briefly. She'd only ever seen Rico in a suit, but now he stood unshaven, a towel wrapped around his waist. From the guarded look on his face the intimacies they had shared last night had been eradicated, and he stared back at her coolly.

'I thought they weren't coming until the funeral.'

'They want to be here for Lily. At least that is what my father said.'

Lily!

A wave of guilt washed over her. She hadn't even given her niece a thought since she had awoken. Catherine turned anguished eyes to his, replacing her cup in the saucer and spilling most of the contents. 'I should ring—'

'I already have,' Rico broke in. 'The bruising is more extensive than they first thought, so they would like to keep her under observation for the next few days. She is fine,' he added, as Catherine opened her mouth to ask. 'The doctor said there is no need for concern; it is just as a precaution. I also get the impression they are assessing her social situation closely. The newspapers are full of it this morning, and though the doctor didn't say as much I have a niggling feeling Antonia has rung from the States and let her feelings be known on the subject. As I feared, it would seem the battle for Lily's future welfare is already gearing up.'

He paused for the longest time. 'Now, we really do have to talk, Catherine.'

She didn't want to talk, didn't want to go over and over things, yet she knew they had to—knew things needed to be sorted and that time wasn't on their side.

'This time tomorrow my family will be here. We cannot stop this from turning ugly. Antonia isn't going to take it lying down, but if we can at least put on a united front with the social workers—if we can at least get the legal ball rolling—we can hopefully prevent Antonia from taking Lily from the hospital.'

'She has no right,' Catherine responded immediately. 'She's not even a blood relative.'

'But my father is,' Rico pointed out. 'And my father will do whatever Antonia tells him, believe me.'

Oh, she did believe him, as much as she might not want to. It had been the same with her own parents, and Catherine swallowed nervously. Only now was the magnitude of what she faced truly registering.

'Look, Rico.' She kept her voice deliberately even. 'I understand your doubts about motives, but that aside, surely you cannot question my suitability? I'm a teacher, I work with children, I'm Lily's aunty…' She reeled off her possible attributes but he remained unmoved. 'Surely after last night, after what we shared…' Her voice trailed off as his face darkened. The fury in his eyes was more painful than any slap, the anger in his voice so visible she recoiled into the pillows, her eyes widening as he spoke, fury blazing in every word.

'I wondered how long it would take you.' He glanced at his heavy gold watch. 'But you even surpassed my expectations. I thought you'd at least last five minutes, but you couldn't even hold out that long.'

'I don't know what you're talking about.'

'You think last night changes anything? Well, it doesn't.' His finger jabbed accusingly at her. 'You warned me yesterday you'd do whatever it takes to get Lily, and I should have bloody listened. So if you think you can use your feminine wiles to win me round you're wrong. We had sex last night. That was all.'

'You really are the limit, Rico.' So blind was her fury,

Catherine didn't even bother to wrap the sheet around her, just stood up out of the bed and reached for a robe, tying the belt furiously around her. She stood before him, bristling with anger. 'Do you really think I orchestrated last night? Do you really think I was lying there hoping you'd come to me? Well, you're wrong. Last night we needed each other. Last night we wanted each other. There was no master plan intended. My God—' Her voice was rising now, and her hand raked through her hair, utterly appalled at his slant on things. 'Sleeping with you was the last thing I expected when I lay down on that bed. You know that, Rico. *You know that,*' she repeated, grabbing his arm and trying to rattle some sense into him. But he flicked it away. 'If we'd thought about it undoubtedly it would never have happened. We didn't even—' Her hand shot up to her lips, trembling, as an impossible thought came into focus.

'Go on.' Rico's voice was like ice, and when Catherine said nothing it was Rico who continued for her. 'We didn't use any precautions, is that what you were about to say?'

She gave a small, worried nod, wincing at the bitterness in Rico's voice. 'Why aren't I surprised that you're not on the Pill, Catherine? Why aren't I surprised that, just like your sister before you, you had unprotected sex—?'

'With a very rich man,' Catherine finished for him, her voice a pale whisper. *'You bastard.'*

Very slowly he shook his head, his eyes menacing as they held hers. One hand touched her cheek, one finger traced her cheekbone, but utterly without tenderness. 'There are no bastards in the Mancini family. You know that, Catherine. Just as Janey did. There are no bastards in the Mancini family because, like the traditional Sicilian family we are, we always pay for our mistakes—and, my God, you'd make me pay, wouldn't you?'

The vileness of his accusation was almost more than she could comprehend. The fact that he could think she would stoop so low ignited the anger that had simmered unattended since the first knock at her door from the police.

'We didn't have sex last night, Rico. We made love. You think I engineered it? You think that while my sister lay in the mortuary I was planning to ensure a link with the Mancinis?'

'You glimpsed wealth.' Rico shrugged. 'For a few hours you saw how your life could be...'

'So I seduced you?' She shook her head fiercely, scarcely able to comprehend what he was accusing her of. 'I summoned you to my bed in the vain hope I might conceive?'

'Just as your sister did with Marco.'

Anger boiled within her, blurred her sense and took away her constraint. 'Haven't Sicilians heard of contraception, Rico? You make out I am some sort of tart when the truth is I have had only two relationships in my life and— as fleeting as it was—you were the second.' She watched his face pale, almost took back what she had just said, lied to save herself. But she was beyond rationality now. Pride intermingled with hurt—a dangerous cocktail. 'So, no, I'm not on the Pill, and I didn't have a condom in my handbag just in case some six-foot-four Sicilian chose to make love to me. You'll have to forgive me for my naivety, Rico, but the question really is, what's your excuse? How come *you* didn't think to take precautions?'

To her utter exasperation he didn't answer.

'Because maybe, just maybe you needed me last night?' Catherine suggested for him. 'Because maybe you needed to be with another person? Needed—'

'I needed sex.' Rico shrugged. 'It helps me sleep.'

'What are you scared of, Rico? Why do you have to sully everything with your own warped take on things?'

'Nothing scares me,' he said proudly, but the lack of conviction in his voice was audible to Catherine.

'Oh, yes, it does. You're scared to believe that last night might actually have been about emotion, that maybe just for a moment in time you needed another human being. But don't worry, Rico, I'm not about to trap you…' Her mind was working overtime, tossing up answers to questions she hadn't even considered. 'There's a pill I can take. I can see a doctor today…'

'There will be no pills.' His eyes narrowed menacingly. 'Put that out of your mind this instant. And, contrary to what you just said, I do need you.'

I do need you. His admission stilled her, but his lack of emotion told her this wasn't going to be the declaration she secretly craved.

'You're right. You are a teacher, a supposed upstanding citizen, and on paper you probably look good. And at the end of the day Lily needs a mother figure in her life.'

'So you won't contest it when I apply for custody?' She could scarcely comprehend it would be that easy, that Rico would give up with barely a fight. But he nodded and she felt her breathing even, her pulse-rate slow down as Rico's eyes met hers and he gave a small smile.

'Of course not.' For a second she relaxed—a stupid move when Rico Mancini was in the room, for he struck like a viper the second her defences were down. 'Why would I fight with my wife when we want the same thing?'

'Your wife?' Bewildered eyes met his, her mouth opening and closing as speech evaded her.

'My wife,' Rico confirmed, a malicious smile carving his strong features. 'That is what you want, after all.'

She moved to deny it, opened her mouth to protest, but the words died on her tongue before they were even formed. Rico was right. That *was* what she wanted—for the last year it had been all she had wanted, all she had secretly craved. But not like this. Never, ever like this.

'Antonia and my father can afford the best lawyers—'

'So can you,' Catherine cut in, but he withered her with a stare.

'This could go on for years. Years,' he repeated, making sure she understood. 'And in that time Lily would be dragged between us. But if you and I unite, if we tell the social workers we are married, that Lily is our first and only priority, we would stand a chance. At the very least I'm sure we'd gain custody, and it would be up to my father and Antonia to try and prove we were not fit.'

'But marriage... I can't believe you're suggesting...'

'Oh, but this isn't a suggestion,' Rico corrected. 'This is what we will do.'

'You can't order me to marry you.' She gave an incredulous laugh. 'You can't drag me up the aisle screaming, Rico.'

'There will be no aisle; there will be no church. I think a quick discreet service would be more appropriate.'

'You really think you've got it all worked out, don't you?'

'Of course I have,' Rico said with annoying patience,

as if he were addressing a petulant two-year-old. 'A young professional couple will certainly appease the family court judges.'

'And I suppose once it's all sorted we arrange a discreet divorce?' Her words were laced with scorn. 'What would happen to Lily then?' Catherine fired. 'I suppose I'd have her during the week and you'd rock up at the weekends?'

'She's not a parcel to be passed around; we will do the right thing by her.'

Catherine shook her head, brown eyes blazing, appalled that he thought it could all be so easy. 'A loveless marriage isn't the right thing, Rico. A convenient divorce isn't the right thing by Lily. She deserves better.'

'And she will get it.' He didn't raise his voice, but something in the icy deliverance of his words told Catherine he meant business. She stepped back slightly, swallowing nervously as he walked over and took her none too gently by the shoulders, fixing her with a menacing stare. 'You are the one who mentioned the word divorce…'

'You can hardly expect me to sign my life away for ever.'

'But that is what happens when you have a child,' Rico pointed out. 'That is the commitment you make. Yesterday you told me you wanted custody, that you wanted to do the right thing by your niece.'

'And I do,' Catherine protested, but not quite so forcibly. 'But, Rico, what is a marriage without love?'

'Ha!' He gave a scornful laugh. 'Love is for fools.' Seeing her shocked face only egged him on further. 'Love is a false state of mind, a fantasy one chooses to live in.'

'You don't believe in love? You don't believe a man and a woman can love each other?' She truly couldn't comprehend the magnitude of his words, but Rico was only too happy to enlighten her.

'Of course they can.' Rico shrugged. 'If they choose to mess up their lives. Look at Janey and Marco. Marco loved her, adored her, and in the end it killed him.'

'But surely...?' Catherine started, but Rico was on a roll now.

'My parents.' He held up his hands then clapped them together. 'Sham! My father and Antonia.' Again he clapped his hands. 'Sham!' Picking up the newspaper, he waved it for an angry moment before tossing it aside. 'I bet this is full of happy couples telling the world how love saved the day. Only this time next year we will be reading how she drank too much, or he hit her.' He clapped his hands together again. 'More shams! Love is for fools, Catherine,' Rico said firmly. 'Love leaves you bleeding. The last thing I want or need in my life is a marriage that is a sham. But this way...'

His eyes narrowed and he eyed her thoughtfully, his voice low and husky but utterly determined as he continued. 'You and I—well, I believe it could work. For centuries my ancestors decided their children's fate, chose their partners for them. There was no love there, no stars in their eyes, no promises that their passion might conquer all—and there was no divorce,' he added triumphantly. 'No fools believing that love would get them through. They made a commitment, worked at their marriage, stuck at it even when times were hard. Maybe the old ways had some merit—'

'Your argument is utterly, utterly flawed,' Catherine interrupted. 'Nobody got divorced in those days unless they were incredibly brave or incredibly rich. But it didn't mean they were happy!' She closed her eyes for a second, massaging her temples as she tried to assimilate Rico's strange logic into the twenty-first century. 'And it isn't our parents choosing a suitable match; it's two people—'

'Two people who want the same thing,' Rico broke in, refusing to move an inch. 'Two people with a vested interest. Love doesn't have to come into it. Love *cannot* come into it. There is too much at stake to lose our heads. This is the right thing,' he added. He was speaking more softly now, but there was no mistaking the determination in his voice. 'Lily needs a mother figure, needs some security, and if we don't unite and present a proper case Antonia and my father will pull out all the stops to ensure a bloody, messy court battle. This is the only way.'

'But the social workers will never believe that our marriage is anything other than one of the shams you so vehemently abhor.'

'Why?' He was almost shaking her now. 'When it isn't one? We both know the rules from the start. No talk of love, no promises we can surely never keep. We will tell them the truth—that there was an instant attraction when we first met a year ago and it flared again last night.' His hands tightened their grip, his face so close she could feel his breath on her cheek. But there was nothing tender in his touch, no affection in the arms that held her. 'Of course we won't shatter their illusions with the seamier side of your nature, Catherine. Naturally they don't need to know that you are merely following in your sister's footsteps, ensuring that your future will be very much taken care off. Apart from that, there is no lie.'

But there was.

One touch, one look from Rico and she was a gibbering mess. With just one show of tenderness, one crook of his finger she had tumbled into bed with him. To deny that love was involved was the biggest lie of all...for Catherine, at least.

'We both care for Lily,' Rico continued, taking her distraction as a motion to continue, 'so we decided to accelerate things—build on our attraction to provide Lily with a stable home. When they hear that you are prepared to give up work—'

'No!' Her response was immediate, a knee-jerk reaction, and the single word came out with more force than she'd intended. As his eyes narrowed Catherine took a deep breath, adjusting her tone, but though her voice was softer there was no mistaking her determination. 'I'm not giving up work, Rico. Maybe I don't make millions, like you do, but my job is equally important. I'm a teacher,' she insisted to her unreceptive audience. 'I can't just walk out mid-term.'

'So teachers don't have children?' Rico asked with annoying logic. 'Are you telling me that teachers around the world plan their pregnancies to fit in with term time?'

'Of course not,' Catherine wailed in frustration. 'You're impossible, Rico,' she shouted. 'Impossible and—and...'

'And what? Come on, Catherine, say what you have to.'

'Contrary to what you choose to believe, Rico, I'm too much of a lady to say what I really think of you. But tell me this—why does it have to be the woman who gives up work? Why *should* it be the woman?'

'Do you really expect me to play house husband!' It

was Rico laughing incredulously now. 'You expect me to walk away from my job to change nappies and go to the park each day to feed the ducks? I am a Mancini,' he said pompously, as if his surname alone closed the discussion. But Catherine refused to be silenced—refused to be intimidated by his arrogant name dropping, even if the name was Rico's own.

'And I'm a Masters.' Her brown eyes flared and Rico's mouth snapped closed. 'And I've worked just as hard as you to get where I am. Maybe I don't make millions, Rico, maybe it won't appear on the news if I decide to walk away from my work. But I have twenty-eight students relying on me to give them an education and I happen to believe I'm making a difference. So don't try to belittle me, Rico. Don't assume I measure my self-worth by your cold standards.'

'I apologise.' For a nanosecond she thought she'd won, thought she had actually made a dent in that cold black heart, but as her eyes flashed to his Catherine knew her victory was short-lived. 'Of course you will work. You will carry on living in your tiny cramped flat and go on living the life you so clearly relish.' Sarcasm dripped off every word as he mercilessly continued. 'But tell me, Catherine, how do you intend to pay for all this? Surely if you work Lily will need full-time care?'

'There are day-care centres,' Catherine retorted. 'Crèches. Lots of women juggle babies with a career!'

'Do you know the price of full-time childcare?'

'Oh, and you do?' Catherine snapped.

'Yes.' His smile was anything but friendly. 'Contrary to what you undoubtedly believe, I pride myself in looking after my staff. Along with their other perks, I decided some years ago to subsidise my working mothers' child-care. It made good business sense: not only do I retain good workers, I am repaid tenfold by their loyalty.'

Damn!

She'd walked into that one. But Catherine consoled herself—it wasn't her fault. Never in a million years could she have seen it coming. Rico Mancini and the reputation that preceded him didn't exactly conjure up the words 'caring' and 'sensitive'. How the hell could she have known he was in the running for the Employer of the Year Award?

But Rico hadn't quite finished twisting the knife.

'Now, call me pedantic if you will, but occasionally I even manage to run an eye over the cheques I sign. So you see, Catherine, I am well aware of the cost of *good* childcare. So I'll ask again—how do you intend to fund this latest acquisition? How are you going to make the jump from single professional woman to single professional working mother?'

'I'll find a way,' Catherine insisted, her mind racing.

'How?'

'I don't know.' Her fingers raked through her hair as she stalled for time, frantically trying to come up with an answer. 'I'll manage—women do. Lily will have some…' Her eyes widened in horror, the steel of the trap Rico had laid for her closing around like a vice.

'Some what, Catherine?'

Colour was whooshing up her cheeks now. Like a trapped animal she darted her eyes around the room, desperate for escape, for some breathing space. The percolator was still dripping, but instead of images of second cups it reminded her of Chinese water torture—relentless questions that demanded answers, Rico twisting and turning the facts until his truth was fashioned.

'Shall I finish that for you, Catherine? Lily will have some money. Is that what you were about to say?' She didn't respond. Not that Rico gave her much option. 'There will be no childcare.' Rico's eyes were menacing now, his hands gripping her wrists as he spelt out the rules. 'That baby has had enough of being palmed off, enough of strangers caring for her. If we do this then we do it right, Catherine. You will have a nanny, a housekeeper—all the staff you need. But Lily's day-to-day care will be provided by you. You will not work.'

'I'm not even discussing this.' Shaking his hand off, she moved away, refusing to look at him as she worked the room, picking up her clothes, trying to locate her shoes, shaking her head in furious disbelief when Rico relentlessly continued.

'We have to show the court commitment. We cannot expect Lily to slot into our lives with no sacrifices.'

'I'm not afraid of sacrifice,' she called over her shoulder, heading into the bathroom and putting her clothes down over the rail, then wailing in frustration as he came up behind her. 'Why aren't I surprised you followed me in? Look, Rico, you do your best and I'll do mine. But there is no way, no way at all, that a marriage between us could work.'

'Why?' He seemed genuinely bemused, genuinely confused at her outright refusal to even consider it. 'We have a niece who needs a home, we are clearly sexually compatible, and there is a chance you are carrying my child, Catherine. I'd say we have three very good reasons to be married—three very good reasons indeed.'

Suddenly Catherine felt panicky and out of control. Actually, not so suddenly—since Rico had reappeared on the scene her responses could hardly be classed as normal. But yesterday, in the daze of grief, watching Lily with a bleeding heart, it had been so easy to say yes, to put up her hand and say of course she was up to it. But now, in the cold light of day, the ramifications were starting to hit home.

This wasn't a puppy or a goldfish she was thinking of taking on while the owners went overseas. This was a baby, a living, breathing baby, and the commitment was for ever. She didn't even have the luxury of nine months to come round to the idea.

Even though Rico never moved she could almost feel the mental snap of his fingers, forcing her into decision. Time was not on their side.

'Why do all the sacrifices have to come from me?' Catherine protested again. 'I happen to like my life, Rico. I like my job, my flat, my social life, and you're asking me to throw it all away.'

'You almost sound convincing. Come on, Catherine, let's not pretend—this is what you've always wanted.'

'You're so pompous.' A sob of frustration fuelled her words. 'So damned sure that this is what I want.'

'Isn't it?' He gave a mocking smile that only fed her fury.

'You tell me to jump and I'm supposed to ask how high! Why should it be me making all the sacrifices? What are you giving up?'

'Oh, there will be sacrifices on my part.' He gave a malicious smile. 'You have every right to expect fidelity.'

His words hurt more than Catherine expected. The

thought of him with another woman was more vile than she could contemplate; jealousy reared its head just at the mere thought.

'I wouldn't just expect it, Rico—I would demand it.'

'So we are agreed, then?' Triumph glittered in his eyes, but faded as Catherine firmly shook her head.

'I have agreed to nothing.' Still she shook her head, but less firmly now, and there was bemusement in her voice as she carried on talking. 'Why, when you clearly think so little of me, Rico, would you want me for your wife? You said yourself I disgust you, and you think all I want from Lily is wealth, so why on earth would you ask me to marry you?'

He stared at her for the longest time, his eyes holding hers. His voice, when it came, was low and measured. 'Keep your friends close, and your enemies closer,' he said softly, but without any trace of tenderness. 'Surely you have heard that saying, Catherine?'

'When did I become the enemy, Rico?' Catherine asked, perplexed eyes scanning his. Her voice was softer now. She was genuinely bemused at the stranger who stood before her now, such a stark contrast to the caring, gentle lover who had held her last night. The man who had reached out in the darkness and kept her afloat through the loneliest hours of her life. 'You know, I almost feel sorry for you, Rico.' Catherine let out a low, hollow laugh. 'I'm starting to think you'd actually prefer for me to be some scheming little gold-digger than— heaven forbid—a real woman, with real feelings.'

'Save it, Catherine,' he clipped. 'You're not impressing anyone. You see, I know what you really think of me. I know how Janey felt about Marco and I can prove it to you.' His words silenced her, his voice so cold that Catherine swore her heart stilled for a second. 'When I saw you at the wedding, Catherine, so proud, so apart from everyone else, I lost my head.' He gave a wry smile. 'Lost my head over a woman I had never even met. All I knew was that I had to talk to you, to get to know you. I've dealt with a million Esthers in my time, yet I used her as an excuse to come over. I *had* to be with you.'

There was a raw note to his voice now, the urgency she had witnessed in her own emotions, and she blinked back at him, listening as his story unfolded. She was scarcely able to believe that this beautiful, beautiful man could have been so moved, so enthralled that he would engineer a meeting with her—scarcely able to believe that, however fleetingly, however transitory, for a slice of time he had adored her.

'*Had* to be with you,' he reiterated, and Catherine felt her heart trip back into action, flickering like a bird against her ribcage as she recalled that night from his perspective. 'What happened in the hotel didn't disgust me, Catherine. What happened in that hotel room was as inevitable as night following day. From the second I laid eyes on you I had to have you, Catherine. There could only ever have been one outcome. It was what happened after that disgusted me.'

A gasp escaped her lips as the words shot out of his mouth. Hazy, best forgotten recollections came cruelly into focus as Rico gave a poor imitation of Janey's voice.

'"Play your cards right, sis, and all this could be yours!"'

Even if the imitation was lousy, each and every shameful word hit its mark. 'Fool I was, I came looking for you,

Catherine—and, my God, I'm glad I did. Glad that I found out in time your true motives. You ask why I stayed away, you ask why I barely went round to see my niece? Well, there is your reason. I knew Janey was using my brother, knew because I'd heard it from her own mouth, and if I'd spent more than five minutes in the same room as Janey I'd have told Marco—told him that his lovely young wife was nothing more than a cheap, conniving tart.'

'I'm sorry.' Appalled, she stammered as she spoke, 'Sorry that you had to hear all that—sorry that you found out that way.'

'I'm not,' Rico responded coolly. 'In fact, though I admit I was disappointed at the time, I'm glad I heard Janey's take on things. 'Those were Janey's words,' Catherine pointed out, but Rico remained unmoved.

'Perhaps, but I didn't hear you putting up too much of an argument.'

'Just because she felt like that it doesn't mean that I do too. And whatever you heard, whatever was said, deep down, I believe that Janey did love him—that somewhere in her heart…' She shook her head slightly. Janey and Marco faded temporarily into the distance as a deeper realisation hit home. 'You came looking for me?'

He gave a curt nod—such a contrast to her stumbling confusion.

'But why?' Catherine begged. 'Why did you come looking for me?' Her mind was skidding into overdrive. Her focus had shifted now, a million rights wronged as a lens clicked and Rico's perspective of the night shifted into focus. Suddenly the world was clearer, finally his indifference was explained—but the hope that shone in her eyes was doused in an instant by the utter contempt in his.

'I was hoping to finish what we'd started.' His lips curled cruelly around each and every word, singeing her hope with a vile hiss as he relentlessly continued. 'What?' he snapped as she recoiled in horror. 'Did you really think it would be for anything else? That Rico Mancini could really want anything more from you?'

His hand snaked along the nape of her neck, his fingers tangling in the mane of hair, pulling her towards him. But there wasn't a shred of tenderness behind his movements, and his eyes were black and cruel, oblivious to her pain as he twisted the knife deeper in her bleeding heart. 'We had unfinished business, Catherine. That is the only reason I came back, and don't ever forget it.'

'So now that's out of the way, can I go ahead and arrange the wedding?' She would not allow him to see how much he had hurt her. Proudly, defiantly she stared back, refusing to be intimidated, refusing to let him see the black hole her heart had once been. 'Well, you certainly know how to propose in style, Mr Mancini.'

'This is the only way you will get Lily, Catherine. The only chance we have against Antonia.'

'So you'll marry a woman you despise for the sake of your niece? A woman you loathe, who under any other circumstances wouldn't be fit to be your wife?'

'Absolutely,' Rico responded, without missing a beat. 'To keep my family safe I would do anything, and Lily is my blood, Catherine.' He smiled then, but there was nothing reassuring about it. 'You put yourself down, though, Catherine. I never said I loathed you, never said I despised you—in fact I have a grudging respect for a woman who knows what she wants, a woman who just like me is prepared to do anything to get it. Your words,' he added, his hand still working the nape of her neck.

Inexplicably, after the most vile of accusations, the cruel deliverance of his speech, a stinging awareness remained, and his touch was a guilty pleasure she would never admit to.

'Despite that rather uptight exterior you're a hot little thing, aren't you, Catherine? Maybe a marriage of convenience might have some compensations after all.'

Her first instinct was to lash out, to slap that taut cheek, to leave tangible evidence of the scorching shame that imbued her. But somewhere deep inside something moved her: somewhere deep inside she knew this was not the real Rico that she was witnessing now. The real Rico had held her last night, and the real Rico was so much more than the man goading her now.

It was the only reason she didn't walk away.

'I will think about it.' As his eyes narrowed and he opened his mouth to argue she broke in and something in her voice told him to keep quiet. 'I will think about it,' she repeated, and his hand dropped to his side. She was almost daring him to disagree, because one word, one more pompous show of arrogance, and this discussion would terminate.

Her back might be to the wall, but she would not be rushed.

'I'm going to the hospital now, Rico. I'm going to speak with the doctors and find out how Lily's doing and then I'm going to spend the day with her. Now, if you want to come with me then that's your prerogative, but I don't want to hear another word about marriage.'

He nodded, a small curt nod, and Catherine let out the breath she had been holding. She gave a small nod of confirmation back, relaxing a touch as she finally gained a semblance of control.

'Of course when making your decision there is one other thing you need to consider.'

The viper was back, striking when her defences were down. Grabbing her wrists and pulling her towards him, Rico ran a hand over her stomach in a curiously possessive gesture.

'If you are carrying my child, Catherine, you can forget any rubbish about being a single parent. You will put out of your mind in an instant any suggestion of a marriage of convenience followed by an amicable divorce. If you are having my baby, this marriage will be for ever.'

CHAPTER FIVE

SHE'D never felt more cold.

Even with the late-afternoon sun shining on her face, even with Lily in her dark-suited arms, soft and warm, smiling and cooing, utterly oblivious to her devastation, Catherine felt as if ice ran through her veins, shivering as she stood at the graveside, barely taking in the words as the coffins were lowered.

The service had passed in a dizzy, nauseating blur. The outpouring of grief she had witnessed from the Sicilian contingent—the frenzy of Marco's relatives, wailing and sobbing, the sheer exhausting emotion that had filled the church and graveside—was such a contrast to the icy reserve that held her together, yet she envied them. Envied their honesty, the cathartic cleansing their outpouring must surely deliver. Instead Catherine's emotions had seemed to implode within her, immobilising her as she stood dry-eyed at the graveside.

The newly dug ground, the vile earthy stench in her nostrils made her want to call out for them to stop, to say that someone, somewhere, somehow had made a terrible mistake, that surely this hadn't been meant to happen, surely some master plan had gone seriously wrong. There was so much left unsaid, so much life still to be lived, so many wrongs to put right. But what good would it do? Even if it had been a mistake, even if the powers that be had this time got it wrong, it was a mistake that would have to be swallowed.

No rewind button to be pushed. Too much had been done to change things.

And somewhere in the abyss of her grief she could feel Rico's hand holding hers, closing in around her icy flesh, squeezing just a little too tight, and she held on, loath to let him know just how much she needed him, but powerless to let go.

'It's over, Catherine.'

The crowd was dispersing, heading back to the endless line of black cars, but still she stood, not wanting that to be it, not wanting Rico's words to be true. It was hard to fathom that this was how it all ended.

'Lily needs to be fed.' It was the first time she had spoken, and her lips shivered around the simple sentence. 'Maybe I should...'

'Jessica will take her home now.' She watched him raise his hand, watched as Jessica came over, smiling awkwardly as she took her charge.

Jessica couldn't yet meet Catherine's eyes, and both women were uncomfortable in each other's presence. The furious row with Janey and Marco was still uppermost in their minds, that last meeting too near to be relegated to history just yet, but too raw and painful to explore with any hope of objectivity. As Catherine handed Lily over she felt guilty at the relief that flooded her. Guilty at how relieved she was that Rico had been able to persuade Jessica to come back and care for Lily. Grateful she wouldn't have to deal with Lily just yet, when it was still taking a supreme effort just to remember to breathe.

Today was too hard.

'We need to face my family now.' Rico broke into her thoughts. 'It is best Lily is not present for this.'

She wasn't up to this today, but Catherine knew they had no choice. Antonia had already made her feelings clear on the subject. The spiteful rows at the hospital were still ringing in her ears, and the venom of her verbal attack when Lily had been discharged into Rico and Catherine's temporary care was as horrible in hindsight as it had been in the present. With a weary nod she walked back to the waiting car, quietly grateful his hand still held hers.

'This isn't going to be pleasant,' Rico warned as she stared blindly out of the window, tears pricking her eyes at the sight of the two lonely mounds of earth, the flowers already wilting in the hot Australian sun.

'None of this is pleasant.'

Under any other circumstances arriving at Carlos Mancini's family home would have been intimidating, to say the least. In Toorak, one of Melbourne's most affluent suburbs, the huge mansion was barely visible from the street. Huge boxed hedges dwarfed the massive black gates that slid open as the limousine approached, but today her mind was too full of all that had been lost to let its opulence overwhelm her. Today the vast stone walls covered with creeping ivy only reminded Catherine of the tombstones in the graveyard and the wreath she had just laid.

Accepting a brandy, Catherine sipped on it. She was not a big drinker, not a drinker, but the warmth of the liquor seeped through her and she braced herself for the inevitable small talk—the awful low murmurs about how well the service had gone, how awful it was to meet under such circumstances. She was determined to hold up her end, for Janey to have a presence here today, no matter how small.

'*Dovè Lily?*' Antonia's voice carried across the large foyer, and even though Catherine spoke not a word of Italian in this instance no translation was needed. Everything stilled, the hushed reverence normally reserved for such events changing instead to a strained silence as every eye turned to Rico and Catherine.

'She was tired.' Rico shrugged, carefully choosing a drink from a passing waiter. 'After all, Antonia, she was only discharged from hospital this morning.'

'Well, she should be here,' Antonia responded, matching Rico's English. 'It's her parents' funeral, after all.'

'No.' Rico's voice was very calm, but there was an edge to it that had the hairs on Catherine's neck standing to attention, and though it galled her she had a certain reluctant admiration for Antonia when she maintained her disdainful glare towards her stepson. 'She shouldn't be here. No six-month-old should have to attend her parents' funeral.'

'That isn't what I meant and you know it, Rico. Your father is in the study; perhaps we should discuss Lily's future there.'

Catherine's mouth dropped open. Oh, she wasn't naïve, and Rico had left no room for doubt that this discussion was imminent, but she'd been sure there would be at the very least an attempt at pleasantries.

'Let's get this over with,' Rico murmured, guiding her by the elbow towards a large imposing room. But Antonia clearly had other ideas, shaking her head the second they entered. '*Questo e solo per famiglia, Rico.*'

'Catherine *is* family,' Rico responded easily, refusing to join Antonia's blatant mind-games. 'She's Lily's aunt.'

'Then she'd better get herself a solicitor.' Antonia flashed him a look that was pure malice, and Catherine privately wondered if this conversation might be best left misunderstood.

'I have no doubt she intends to,' Rico said, with a note of dryness that was clearly for Catherine's benefit. 'But given the fact that Lily has been entrusted into both Catherine's and my care, I suggest it would be prudent if she stays and polite to have this discussion in English.'

'You've only been granted temporary care,' Antonia corrected. 'The social worker was very clear about that when I spoke with her; this isn't finished by a long shot. Heaven only knows what lies the two of you fed that social worker. Why on earth she would think you could provide better care than Carlos and I is beyond me.' This time it was Catherine who was the recipient of Antonia's withering stare. 'Don't think I don't know where you're coming from, young lady.' Her lips curled into a sneer. 'You're a guttersnipe, just like your sister.'

She flicked her eyes away, clearly ready to move on to seemingly more important things, but for the first time since entering the house, Catherine found her voice.

'I can understand that you have issues with me, Antonia.' The voice was shaky, but her resolve was steel. 'However, Marco wasn't the only person buried this afternoon. It was my sister's funeral also, and, given that it is my sister's daughter we're discussing, I'd ask that you all show Janey some respect, at least where Lily's concerned.'

Her words seemed to reach Antonia. Her expression

softened slightly and she gave a brief nod that Catherine took as an apology before turning her attention back to Rico.

'Your father and I have discussed this at length,' Antonia stated. 'In fact we've barely slept since the accident.'

'How exhausting for you,' Rico drawled, but his sarcasm was wasted.

'It has been,' Antonia agreed, fishing a small lace handkerchief from her heavily tanned bosom and dabbing at a tear Catherine couldn't see. 'But that's not the issue. The issue is Lily's welfare.'

'Agreed,' Rico said, but his expression was anything but receptive.

'Lily needs security.' Antonia looked over to her husband, who smiled warily back. 'And your father and I are the ones who can give her that.'

'Are you sure it isn't the other way round?' Rico's voice cut like a knife, his black stare withering, and Catherine was eternally grateful that for once she wasn't the recipient of his simmering anger.

'This has nothing to do with money,' Antonia insisted, gesturing to the opulent study, with a beautifully manicured hand, then fingering the heavy jewels around her neck. 'Your father and I are hardly in the poor house.'

'But you *are* heading into financial trouble.'

'Don't be ridiculous!' Antonia's eyes were bulging and her well made-up face reddened as Rico eyed her disdainfully.

'I'm not the one being ridiculous,' Rico replied without a trace of emotion. 'I'm not the one jetting around the world in my own private plane with an entourage of staff.

I'm not the one flying to Paris to update my wardrobe or deciding on a whim to head over to New York to see the tennis.'

Even in her numb state of grief Catherine felt a surge of shock at the sheer lavishness of Antonia's existence.

'You're living beyond your means,' Rico said, his voice darker now.

'How would you know?' Antonia flared, but Rico merely shrugged and for the first time addressed his father.

'I know because I bought out your portion of the business. I know because I still do your accounts, Dad, and at the end of the day valuing properties is my bread and butter. As nice as this is, as divine as your Queensland holiday home might be, and all the other little nest-eggs you've got stashed away, the simple fact of the matter is that you cannot afford this lifestyle indefinitely. Some day in the not too distant future something will have to give.' The harshness left his voice then, and a note of exasperation crept in as he implored Carlos to listen. 'Have you read any of the paperwork I gave you, Dad?'

'I haven't had time.' Carlos Mancini's voice was still heavily accented. 'And today is not the day for money talk. Today I lay my son to rest.'

'Fair enough.' Rico nodded, but from previous experience Catherine knew the conversation wasn't over—knew Rico wasn't going to just walk away now. 'If it really isn't about money then let's make a deal before the solicitors get involved—before this leaves the family and becomes open gossip for every journalist in Australia.'

He paused for an age before continuing. The heavy clock on the mantelpiece ticked so slowly Catherine would have sworn it was faulty, so long did each passing second drag.

'We all agree that Lily's money stays in trust for her until she's twenty-one, and that whoever gets custody finances Lily's upbringing by their own means.'

'Lily will need an education.' Antonia was choosing her words carefully but her agitation was palpable. 'You can hardly expect your father and I to fund—'

'The sad thing is,' Rico broke in, 'I don't expect a thing from the two of you. The saddest part of this whole discussion is that Lily is nothing more than a means to an end for you, Antonia.'

Catherine simply didn't know where to look, it was horrible watching as Antonia flushed ever darker, her mouth pursing. Rico's father was fishing in his suit for a handkerchief and wiping his brow, and she felt sorry for him, remembering that at the end of the day, Carlos Mancini had buried his youngest son today. But Rico clearly wasn't taking that into consideration, for he didn't let up, was ruthless in his pursuit as he carried on talking. 'Lily would provide a nice little pension for the pair of you, as well as getting you out of the hole you've dug yourself into.'

'Oh, we didn't dig,' Antonia soon recovered and stood up, her eyes bulging as she faced her stepson, veins standing out in her neck as she choked out the words. 'You buried us, Rico. You put us in this hole the day you bought your father out of the business for a pittance.'

'Hardly a pittance,' Rico drawled but his icy reserve only exacerbated Antonia's fury.

'You knew the company was about to take off.' Antonia was practically purple now. 'You knew the fortune it was going to make, and yet you bought out your brother and father for a tenth of what you would now. And you have the gall to stand there and gloat, the tenacity to breeze in and tell us that we're in financial trouble when *you're* the one with blood on your hands.'

Catherine's eyes shot to Rico as she waited for him to say something, for him to defend himself against Antonia's vile accusations. But he just stood there, his face impassive, not a bead of sweat on his brow, and not for the first time Catherine wondered what she had got herself into, wondered at the lengths Rico was clearly prepared to go to in order to claim what he assumed was rightly his.

'So far, Antonia, you've said two things that merit comment.'

Finally, Catherine thought. Finally he's going to put her in her place, clear the slur on his name. But the hope that flared was extinguished as Rico continued.

'The issue *is* Lily's welfare, and, yes, Lily, *does* need security, which I'm more than capable of providing.'

'You!' Antonia sneered. 'A man who has had more girlfriends than I've had hot dinners? A man who spends fifteen hours a day in an office? When are you supposed to see her, Rico? Are you intending to e-mail her a couple of times a day? Read her a bedtime story over the telephone?'

'And you're such an expert on parenting suddenly, Antonia?'

This time Rico's sarcasm didn't go unnoticed.

'You were eighteen when I married your father, Rico. Hardly an age for fairytales and nights around the fire with a cup of cocoa. So cut it with the sob stories. I was good to you.'

'You were good for nothing, Antonia!' Rico's voice was pure venom. 'And, yes, I was eighteen. Yes, I was old enough to get on with my life, to walk away from the woman who had destroyed not only my mother's marriage but ultimately her life. But Marco was twelve—a twelve-year-old boy you treated like dirt on your shoe. You moved in and he was shipped out to boarding school the next month. *The next month,*' he repeated, emotion finally rearing its head, his voice a loud roar. 'Is that what you intend for Lily?'

'She's a baby,' Antonia retorted. 'She's years away from school. It's not even an issue at the moment. You're not having her, Rico. I'll sell the plane if I have to, but I'll fight you till the end for her.' Her eyes met Catherine's, locked on them for an uncomfortable moment, and suddenly everything didn't seem quite so crystal-clear any more. The picture Rico had painted of a money-hungry woman was suddenly not quite so plausible. 'Your sister would want the best for her daughter—surely you can see that?'

Catherine gave a small nod.

'Let's put the money aside for a moment.' Antonia's voice bordered on reasonable, and again Catherine nodded, determined to hear all sides, to make a rational decision when all the cards were on the table. Lily's future was too precious for egos and finances to get in the way. 'Children should have two parents. That might sound old-fashioned, but I firmly believe it—as I'm sure the courts do—'

'For once we agree on something,' Rico's voice broke in, and Catherine shot him a furious look.

'Antonia was talking, Rico. I think we should at least hear what she has to say.'

'I'm tired of listening to her crap.' Taking Catherine's hand, he held it for a moment, slowly turning it over in his palm before holding it up. 'Notice anything?' His malevolent tones had shivers running down Catherine's spine, and there was nothing tender in the way he held her. 'Aren't you going to congratulate us, Father?' When Carlos just sat there in stunned silence he addressed his stepmother. 'Antonia? Aren't you going to welcome the newest addition to the Mancini family?'

'You see, you're right Antonia. Children *do* deserve two parents, and I figured with you damaging my reputation, coupled with the hours I put in at the office—well, it might go against me if I were in sole charge. But given I've got a loving wife at home—a loving, educated wife, I hasten to add, with not a single skeleton in the cupboard—well, I'm sure the courts will understand that I need to provide for my family. I'm sure the courts will have no hesitation in giving Catherine and I full custody.'

The room was icy cold. Antonia was opening and closing her mouth like a goldfish as Rico's hand snaked around Catherine's face and he planted a kiss on her cheek in a curiously triumphant gesture before addressing his family. 'Antonia, Father—' Rico smiled in turn at them both. 'Allow me to introduce my wife.'

'Your wife?' The incredulity in Antonia's voice wasn't born of affection; Catherine could almost taste her disgust as it permeated the room. 'When did this happen?'

'This morning.' Rico's voice was insolent. 'You'll understand there wasn't exactly time to send out invitations, and naturally we don't expect a present, but surely congratulations should be in order?'

'Never!'

Antonia was shuddering with an unleashed fury which Rico clearly wasn't going to hang around to witness. As he stalked out of the room, Catherine knew her supposed place was by his side, but her legs were leaden as she turned to go. She was truly torn by what she had witnessed.

'He's using you.' Antonia almost ran to catch up with her. Pulling at Catherine's suit, she turned her around, and Catherine waited—waited for confrontation, for accusations of what she didn't know. But more bewildering was a look from Antonia that bordered on sympathetic, a touch that was almost maternal as she squeezed Catherine's arm. 'Maybe you think you're using him as well, Catherine. Perhaps you've agreed to use each other. But I'm telling you: you won't come out of this unscathed.'

'Please, Antonia,' Catherine warned her, 'don't threaten me.'

'I'm not threatening you, my dear.' Antonia shook her head. 'It's not me that you have to fear; I only want what's best for Lily.'

'So do I.' Catherine's throat was dry, her mouth like sandpaper, and she could see Rico out of the corner of her eye, waiting impatiently for her to join him. But still she held her ground. 'And I truly believe that this is the best way.'

'Can I at least see her?' Tears were filling Antonia's eyes now, and Catherine was appalled at what she had been reduced to. She had read about grandparents being kept from their grandchildren, had moaned with her colleagues about children being used as a weapon in bitter custody battles, and to think she was capable of it truly appalled her. 'Please don't keep us away from her while the court case goes on. Whatever happens between the families, surely we should still be able to see her.'

'Of—of course,' Catherine stammered. 'Lily needs people who love her.'

'And I do love her.' Antonia gulped. 'Whatever Rico says about me, I do love her. All I'm asking is that you remember that.'

Oh, she didn't want to remember that—didn't want the rules to suddenly change. It had all been so much easier when Antonia was the enemy—a cold, heartless woman who would stop at nothing—but suddenly she didn't look so cold. Right now she looked like a grandmother having her heart stamped on.

'I have to go,' Catherine said. 'Rico is waiting…'

'It's Rico you need to watch out for,' Antonia warned, her eyes boring into her, almost mesmerising in their clarity. 'He's using you, and when he's finished with you he'll toss you aside, the same as he did with his father, the same as he did with his brother. You'll be left with nothing.'

'I'm Lily's aunty,' Catherine said, with a conviction that wavered as Antonia shook her head slowly.

'You're a pawn, darling. A pawn in one of Rico's games.'

CHAPTER SIX

'I KNOW it all seems a bit strange, but you'll soon get used to it.'

Catherine didn't even deign to give a response as she clipped along the marble entrance hall in her high heels, her dark suit matching her sombre mood. Antonia's words were still ringing in her ears as she tried to fathom the new world she now inhabited.

And he watched.

Watched from a distance as she explored her new surroundings, quietly proud of her detached dignity as she adjusted to yet another new page in the book of her life, again faced the challenges the world seemed only too willing to provide this resilient woman.

You have to let her come to you.

How many times over the last days had he heard that?

Every time Lily had arched her back, sobbed in protest as he held out his arms to her, the social worker had repeated those words. 'She's confused, scared—it's all too much for her to take in. If you can just be there for her, and try not to expect too much, then in time she'll come to you.'

But it wasn't Lily worrying him now; tonight his concern was purely for Catherine.

How he longed to go over to his new bride, to shower that pale, strained face with kisses, to make things better with just a smile. But this wasn't a baby to be won over with a smile; this was a woman…

In every sense of the word, Rico thought, then attempted a retraction, mentally slamming closed a window that simply couldn't be opened tonight.

He wanted to tell her—tell her what was in his heart—but surely now wasn't the time. Catherine had enough to deal with, without clouding the issue with his pointless declarations.

A loveless marriage.

That was what they had agreed and that was how it must be. For now at least.

Yet no matter how he fought it, no matter how he tried to feign aloofness, still he found himself admiring those legs that seemed to go on for ever, silhouetted by her sheer stockings as she walked the length of the house. He took in the soft curve of her stomach, so much more appealing than the flat, concave gamines he usually dated.

But though he adored her with his eyes, they narrowed in concern as she made her way back to the entrance hall. She faced him head-on for the first time that day, and he couldn't help but notice the dark smudges under eyes that had lost all their sparkle, the luscious hair tied back in a severe knot. Only her lips added a splash of colour, but even they seemed to have paled, and he ached, physically ached to take her into his arms and kiss away all the hurt, to somehow let her know that he understood the hell of today—the funeral, the awful confrontation with his family. But something in her stance told him he was neither wanted nor needed.

'I'd better check on Lily.' Even her voice seemed to have lost its fire. 'Listless' was the word that sprang to mind. Her eyes didn't even flick to his as she headed for the stairs.

'Jessica said she was sleeping,' Rico pointed out. 'Maybe it's best not to disturb her.'

'Jessica's the nanny.' Catherine shrugged. 'I thought nighttime kisses and fairy stories were my department.'

'Catherine.' He came up behind her, taking the stairs two at a time till he stood beside her, one hand reaching for her shoulder. But he saw her stiffen before he even made contact and pulled it away. 'You've just lost your sister, moved out of your home—'

'And just got married!' Her eyes glinted dangerously at him. 'You failed to mention the fact we got married this morning, Rico. But then why would you? It was hardly the ceremony of the century.'

'Which was what you wanted,' Rico pointed out. 'What you insisted upon.'

And it had been, Catherine conceded. But only to herself. She'd never been one of those women who'd dreamed since childhood about her wedding day, but a draughty, bland register office in the middle of the city, a ceremony snatched between meetings with lawyers and funeral preparations, certainly hadn't been envisaged either.

'I just didn't expect it to be so—'

'Look,' Rico quickly interrupted, 'I know it wasn't much of a wedding—I know that it was all a bit rushed. If you want, we can do it again—do it properly. When things have settled down we can have the wedding you want, the wedding you deserve. I'll get my secretary to find you the best wedding planners; they can put you on to designers, anything you want...'

He was trying to help, Catherine told herself. Rico Mancini was used to waving a chequebook to fix things, used to plastering over cracks. But her pain ran too deep.

He simply didn't get it.

He'd probably never get it.

The bland surroundings, the lack of grandeur, her crumpled clothes, the impassive celebrant—they didn't matter a jot.

Had Rico only loved her, had his eyes adored her as he'd taken her as his wife, had his hand only reached for hers as they'd signed the register, the wedding would have been all she'd ever hoped for.

Her wedding would have been magical.

'I'm going to check on Lily.'

'Leave Lily for now.' Rico was insistent. 'Jessica seems very responsible and her room is just next door to Lily's. Why don't you come and have a drink?'

'I don't want a drink.'

'Well, a bath, then.'

She gave a low laugh. 'I would, except I don't even know where the bathroom is.'

'Catherine, please.' She could hear an impatient note to his voice and gave a wry shake of her head—her allotted two minutes of understanding were clearly up.

'What's wrong, Rico?' Accusing eyes turned to his, for even though she was as much a participant as Rico, a willing partner in the sham they had engineered, somehow she couldn't help but blame him.

Blame him for not loving her back.

'Aren't I playing the part of new bride to your satisfaction? Are you disappointed I didn't want to be carried over the threshold to satisfy the photographers? Were you hoping I might have a nice bath and then slip into something more comfortable?'

'Of course not—' Rico started, but Catherine hadn't finished.

'You've got what you wanted, Rico. I've kept up my end of the deal. But don't for one second expect me to be happy about it.'

Even as she spoke Catherine regretted her harsh words. She didn't want to be like this, didn't want to be mooching around like a surly teenager, making this uncomfortable situation worse for both of them. But it was as if she couldn't help herself.

Antonia's dreadful accusations were still buzzing in her ears. How she longed to escape for a few days, to check out of the world and digest all that had happened, assimilate it into some sort of order—something she could deal with. But at her own bidding she was a mother now. And not one part of her life was familiar. Her possessions had been cleared from her flat in a single day, compassionate leave arranged from work with one phone call—even her name was different: Catherine Mancini.

Catherine Mancini, who lived in a huge, imposing house, with servants and nannies. Catherine Mancini, who had a baby to care for. Catherine Mancini, wife to a husband who under any other circumstances wouldn't have deigned to marry her.

'Leave Lily,' he said again, and the tone of his voice told Catherine he wasn't about to be argued with. 'If you wake her now it will take ages to settle her, and we're both exhausted.'

'Fine.' Her mouth barely moved. 'Maybe I will have a

bath after all, and then I think I'll go to bed. Could you show me where I'll be sleeping?'

'Of course.' He led her up the stairs, his hand resting gently on tense shoulders that stiffened even more as he pushed open the large mahogany door. He registered her sharp intake of breath as she eyed the vast bed, the massive floor-to-ceiling windows that took in the shimmering Melbourne skyline. 'I will even run a bath for you.'

Run a bath. He made it sound such a supreme effort, and for Rico it probably was, Catherine mused as he walked across the room. No doubt this was a first. She watched as he stood for a moment by the vast sunken spa, eyeing the bottles of oil, then flicking a switch. She stood, seemingly transfixed by the swirling bubbles but struggling against a surge of panic, wishing more than Catherine had ever wished in her life that she could do it. Could slip off her clothes with the confidence his numerous other lovers had undoubtedly had, smile up at him through her eyelashes and suggest he join her. But she felt as if her feet had been nailed to the floor, a shadow of what Rico undoubtedly expected his wife to be—a mere solution to a problem, a wife of convenience in every sense.

'There must be another room.' She ran a tongue over her dry lips, watched his eyes narrow, the muscles on his face quilting as he turned to face her. 'I mean, it might make things easier for both of us...'

'Easier?' His voice was menacingly quiet and she had to strain to catch it over the noise of the running water. 'You think my wife sleeping down the hallway will make things easier? Tell me how so, Catherine?'

'I think it would be easier if we had a bit of space. We both know this isn't a true marriage; we both know we don't…' She swallowed nervously. Lies were hard work, even at this dangerous stage.

'Don't love each other?' Rico finished the sentence for her, the words snapping out through his taut lips, and the air crackled with tension as Catherine gave a nervous nod, consoling herself that it was a lie by omission only.

To love each other took commitment from both sides, a commitment Rico had vowed he would never give. But though she loved him she hated him too—hated his presumption, his arrogance, the way he walked over people he should care about.

The questions that had saturated her mind since the wake could be voiced now; answers were needed before she could even contemplate continuing this charade. Forcing herself to take a calming breath, finally she spoke. 'Is it true what Antonia said? Did you know that the business was going to take off when you bought out your brother and father?'

He didn't answer for a moment, and when he did despite his blithe response Catherine knew she'd hit a nerve. 'I knew it was a possibility.'

'But Antonia said—'

'Forget Antonia.' His voice was like the crack of a whip, his nonchalance disappearing as Catherine pressed on. 'She is poison—evil. I told you not to listen to a word she says.'

'And that's supposed to be enough for me?' Catherine flared. 'You tell me not to listen and I'm supposed to comply? Am I not allowed to form my own opinions, Rico? Are you going to remind me again of the good old days, when wives took their husbands' opinions as gospel? The good old days when wives meekly complied with the master's orders?'

'You are twisting my words; I am telling you that woman is no good,' Rico growled, grabbing her wrist and pulling her towards him to force her to listen. But Catherine pulled her hand away, standing tall and proud, looking him square in the eyes.

'I heard you the first time, Rico.' Catherine was shouting now. 'And you can scream it from the rafters, swear it to be true, but so far all I see is a grandmother with her back to the wall—a grandmother fighting to raise her orphaned grandchild.'

'Step-grandchild,' Rico corrected, but Catherine refused to buy it.

'Now who's twisting words, Rico? We'll never be Lily's biological parents, yet that doesn't mean we won't love her as if we were! And you still haven't answered my question. Did you pay off your brother and father knowing that the business was about to explode into an empire?'

'It was years ago.' Rico's hands were working furiously now, tossing in the air with exasperated gestures, and again he reminded her of a lion—but trapped now, pacing the cage restlessly, his simmering anger ready to explode. 'Why the hell do we have to drag it up? Why go into things that don't have any bearing on the here and now? They didn't have to sell.'

'The same way I didn't have to marry you?' She gave a low, mirthless laugh. 'I bet you ensured that they had no choice but to sell—the same way you gave me no choice. And despite what you say it does have a bearing on us. How you treated your family in the past is a pretty good indicator of how you're going to treat me in the future, Rico. There's a lot of unfinished business there. A lot of pain—'

'Oh, there's pain,' Rico said darkly, his eyes narrowing as he looked at her. 'But go on, Catherine. Finish what you were saying.'

She swallowed hard. Something in his voice merited deeper exploration, but she had to see this through, could not be dragged from the path again by Rico's clever bidding. 'I'm not sure I want to be married to a man who could cheat his own family.'

A compressed hiss escaped his lips. So savage was the fury in his eyes that Catherine braced herself for impact, for that incurable Latin temperament to bubble over into a blind torrent of rage.

All of that she could have dealt with.

Could have fought his fire with her own.

Only it never came. For an age he didn't answer, just calmly walked over and flicked off the taps she had forgotten were even running, and when he straightened up, when he turned to address her, his voice was incredibly even, his icy demeanor more chilling than any heated confrontation.

'You make it sound as if you still have a choice, Catherine. You make it sound as if you are still considering the proposal I made back at the hotel.' He held up his left hand, the heavy gold band she had placed there catching the light as he crossed the room towards her. 'Might I remind you that we have a legally binding commitment to each other? The register you signed wasn't a birthday card, or a casual letter you can rip up and forget about.' His face was so close she could feel every word he uttered skim along her cheek, feel the tension in every muscle as he stood before her, body taut, eyes blazing. 'You are my wife now, Catherine, with all that that entails.'

'Surely you can't expect us to share a bed? Surely after all that's gone on you don't expect us to sleep together?'

'Back at the hotel I remember us sharing a bed together. I don't remember you needing space then!'

'That was then,' Catherine retaliated. 'I was confused, lonely…' Pleading eyes begged him to understand, and if he'd just taken her in his arms, told her it was all okay, that it wasn't just for appearances' sake he wanted her in his bed, she'd have gone to him without hesitation— would have settled, even, for a convincing lie. But Rico was a closed book. Not one flicker of his face betrayed how he was feeling. Every emotion was guarded fiercely behind the mask he so readily wore.

'I can't do it, Rico. Please don't make me.'

Her plea was genuine, for with one crook of his finger she knew she would dissolve like jelly in hot water—fall into his arms and betray herself with the words he didn't want to hear. Or maybe he did, Catherine realised.

After all, if she loved him, he won.

'We don't have a choice.' He nodded to the window. 'Did you notice the press when we came home, Catherine? Are you foolish enough to think that they've got their pictures and gone home now?' He gave a mocking laugh. 'They don't believe in fairytales any more than I do, and each and every one of them will want to be the first to prove their point—lights flicking on in the guest room will do just that. And if by some chance we manage to fool them on that score, how long do you think it will be before one of the staff decides Christmas should come a bit early?'

'I don't understand…'

'Trust no one, Catherine,' Rico said darkly, a mocking smile curving on his lips. 'Except maybe me.'

'And that's supposed to make me feel better?' Her pulse was pounding in her temples now—not gently, though. A nauseating throbbing would be a more apt description. Her hand moved up, massaging her temples, and she wondered how best to play this.

'Don't tell me…' His voice was dripping with sarcasm. 'You're getting a headache?'

'Isn't that what wives normally get?' Catherine bit back, but Rico's riposte was just as swift.

'I believe so. Though generally after the marriage is consummated.'

A low laugh escaped her pale lips. 'Worried the contract is not quite legally binding, Rico? Are you worried that until we've slept together I might be able to ask for an annulment?'

'I never worry about small details. Why would I when I have an army of solicitors to do it for me? And I believe, off the top of my head, that a request for an annulment wouldn't stand up too well in court when only days before the wedding the bride was not only sleeping with the groom but begging for it.'

'I never begged.'

'Oh, no?'

He never moved, his eyes stayed fixed and not a muscle flickered in his body, but she could almost taste the sudden sexual tension. The suggestion in his words was enough to cast her mind back until she could almost see her head on the pillow, thrashing in frenzied passion as she wept for him to enter her, and she knew he was thinking it too. The knowledge caused a ripple of lust to dart through her traitorous body—just the memory of his touch was enough to instigate instant arousal.

'That's not how I remember it, Catherine.'

His words should have shamed her, but she was beyond that now. His scorn should have hurt, but Catherine was beyond pain. She had buried her sister today, sworn at Janey's graveside she would do her best for Lily, and if standing tall and proud, quelling her fears and fighting back was the order of the day, then somehow she'd do it. This was Rico Mancini she was up against—a man who would use her to further his cause. She had to remember that, had to keep her head however much she wanted to lose it, had to stay strong.

For Janey and for Lily.

'Then I'm not the only fool in this room.' The derisive note in her voice, the clarity of her speech, surprised even Catherine. And when she saw the dart of confusion in his eyes it was all that was needed to spur her on further.

One tiny victory when all had seemed lost.

'Contrary to your orders, I haven't quite burnt all my bridges—I didn't hand in my notice, Rico, I'm on compassionate leave. So I can walk back into my old life at any given moment.' She stepped back slightly; the fire was back in her eyes now, a soft pink dusted her pale cheeks and her chin set determinedly as she carried on talking. 'But then why would I bother when there's always the divorce card to play? Even the *ex* Mrs Mancini would have more clout in a courtroom than Miss Catherine Masters.'

'That's why you said yes?' Rico's voice was a pale whisper.

'That's the *only* reason I said yes,' Catherine said firmly.

'You wanted me that night,' he insisted, but though his voice was resolute there was flicker of doubt in his eyes.

'I wouldn't be so sure, Rico.' As she turned Catherine smiled softly at him, but it was a smile laced with danger, a curious cocktail of seduction and menace.

The gentle, sweet woman was gone now; instead a bewitching temptress smiled back at him. He stood frozen, watching transfixed as she loosened her hair from its confines, pulled off her jacket and worked the buttons of her black lace blouse, undressing slowly, but utterly ignoring him at the same time, absolutely refusing to let him see the effect he was having on her, determined not to be intimidated.

For the first time in their strange relationship Catherine knew the power of being a woman, learnt the lessons her mother and Janey had unwittingly imparted.

Knew for once she had the valuable upper hand.

'What proud Sicilian would like his lack of sexual prowess played out in court? What proud Sicilian would want the world to know that one night with a woman was enough to make her ensure it was the last?'

Unzipping her skirt, she let it fall around her ankles. Under any other circumstances she would have felt stupid, utterly stupid, standing in stockings and high heels, her creamy breasts spilling out of black lace. But his well-cut suit wasn't enough to hide his furious arousal, and Catherine flicked a superior eye downwards before turning her triumphant gaze back to him as she discarded her bra.

'You lie.' He cursed the words at her, but she deliberately didn't flinch. 'You enjoyed every moment.'

'Did I?' Slowly she walked over to the bath, and slowly she lowered herself in—grateful for the heated water as an excuse for her flaming skin, grateful for the bubbles that covered her jutting nipples. 'I'm sure Marco was equally convinced when Janey called out his name.'

His eyes found hers then.

'You bitch.'

'Why act so surprised, Rico? All along you've accused me of being a gold-digger, all along you've insisted I'm only here for the money, and yet now you've finally got me to admit it you don't seem very pleased all of a sudden.' Dragging her eyes away, she concentrated for an age on the bottles, before selecting one and massaging its contents into her hair. He stood rigid beside the bathtub, his face livid, anger blazing in every taut muscle.

'Lily is my sole priority, Rico. Not this marriage and definitely not you. And if you think you can use me as some sort of pawn in your game and I'll just comply—'

'You believe Antonia?' Rico demanded. 'After everything I said, still you choose to believe her?'

'I believe no one,' Catherine said resolutely. 'But believe this, Rico. If you think you can brush me off like some smudge on your suit when it all dies down, that I'll walk away without a fight, then you'd better think again. Catherine Masters has long gone now, I'm Catherine *Mancini*, with everything the name entails.'

CHAPTER SEVEN

SHE waited for morning.

Lying in the massive bed, feeling the bristling hatred emanating from him, she ached, literally ached to go over to him, to lay her head on his chest and to feel his arms around her, to take back all she had said. But there was too much at stake, too much to lose in a weak moment. So instead she lay there, the room as light as day as the full moon drifted past the massive windows, listening to the creaking house, every nerve taut as finally his breathing evened out.

One heavy arm moved towards her, almost instinctive in its directness, caressing the curve of her waist until she turned towards him. She'd never seen him asleep before, never witnessed the beauty of his face without tension. The taut mouth was relaxed, full, sensual lips slightly parted, dark eyelashes fanning his haughty cheeks, and he looked younger, softer, but so desirable she had to bite back the urge to kiss him, to place her lips on his. Instead she adored him with her eyes, stealing this time away from his accusing glare to absorb his beauty, to capture the delicious image of a husband who was hers in name only.

Her eyes drifted down to the rumpled sheet that lay precariously over his manhood, and she had to clench her fists, such was her desire to move it, to unwrap the parcel and claim the prize. And what terrified her most was that she knew, just knew, he would respond. There was an undeniable attraction that overrode all else. In sleep, his body would yield to her, that tumid length would harden, would awake in her hands. But what then...?

Could a marriage survive on sex alone? Was attraction enough to carry them through whatever lay ahead? Oh, *she* had love—but was it enough for both of them?

Such was her pain that for a moment she thought the piercing cry that filled her ears had come from her own lips. It took a moment to register it was Lily.

Quietly she slipped from Rico's embrace. Wrapping her bath towel around her, she crept down the passage, arriving at the nursery door just as Jessica did.

'I'm sorry she woke you, Mrs Mancini. I was just warming a bottle. I'll take care of her now.'

'I'll do it, Jessica. I don't mind getting up to her at night.'

'Oh!' Jessica gave her a slightly startled look. 'Janey always...' Her voice trailed off and Catherine did nothing to resurrect the conversation, the words hanging in the air as she opened the nursery door and padded in. She was curiously nervous about what exactly it was she was supposed do, and smiled awkwardly at Lily, who had her arms outstretched, tears streaming down her angry red cheeks as she sobbed in anguish.

'Hush,' Catherine begged, picking her up and trying to cuddle her. But despite her best efforts she simply refused to take the bottle, refused to be comforted. It was almost a relief when a hesitant Jessica reappeared at the door.

'I think she wants you,' Catherine admitted, curiously defeated by Lily's rejection, tears glittering dangerously in her eyes as Jessica came over.

'It isn't me Lily wants; she just likes to be changed first.' Registering Catherine's frown, Jessica gestured to the change table. 'She likes her nappy changed before she has her bottle, then she settles right down.'

'Of course.' Catherine's movements were wooden her gestures awkward as she laid Lily down on the changing table, and even though she wanted Jessica to go, even though she wanted her fumbling to be unwitnessed, Catherine was silently terrified of being left alone with Lily; the full weight of the responsibility that she had fought for, starting to descend on her tense shoulders. 'All these poppers.' She let out a nervous laugh, pulling the legs of Lily's baby suit closed over the clumsily applied nappy.

'You'll soon get used to them,' Jessica said kindly. 'I'll leave you to it, then.'

It took a moment to register she hadn't gone. Only when Catherine looked up did she realise Jessica still stood there.

'Mrs Mancini?' Her voice was hesitant, and under any other circumstances Catherine would have moved to reassure her. But, knowing what was coming, she simply couldn't do it. 'About that night—about the row we had with Janey...'

Deliberately Catherine didn't turn her head; deliberately she concentrated on the poppers.

'I feel so guilty.'

'You have nothing to feel guilty about.' Catherine's voice was high, her gestures subtly dismissive as still she focused on the blessed poppers. 'Neither of us have anything to feel guilty about, come to that. Janey and Marco were out of line, and something had to be said.'

'But if I hadn't walked out on them that morning...'

'This isn't your fault.' Finally she met her employee's eyes. 'And going over it doesn't change a thing. It's Lily who is important now.'

'I know,' Jessica mumbled. 'Except...'

Oh, God, she didn't need this now—didn't want to be standing here at two a.m., lifting the lid on Pandora's Box. But she wasn't quite ready to close it either.

'Except what?'

'Janey begged me to stay.' Tears were streaming down Jessica's cheeks unstopped, and Catherine felt like joining her. But she knew she had to be strong if ever she were to survive. 'Janey swore she was going to change, that they both were. She said...'

'That thing's would be different?' Catherine shook her head ruefully. 'That it really was the last time? Well, let me tell you, Jessica, I've lost count of how many times Janey said the same to me—lost count of the times she swore things were about to change. The last thing either of us deserves is another dose of guilt. Janey made her own choices, and unfortunately we're the ones living with them. You have *nothing* to feel guilty about.'

She watched as Jessica nodded, saw her dejected shoulders as she turned to leave the nursery, and knew she had said nothing to comfort her.

'Jessica?' Catherine called her back. 'This wasn't your fault and it wasn't mine. I don't want to hear another word about what was said that night, or what happened the morning after. We did nothing wrong.'

If only she could believe it.

Blinking back tears as the door closed on Jessica, Catherine settled back in the rocking chair she and Rico had hastily chosen, along with the rest of the nursery furniture. It felt like a film set—everything new, everything staged for tonight's main show—and at that moment Catherine felt like the worst actress in the world.

Lily let out a low whimper which Catherine quickly countered, pulling the baby in closer. But she could barely feign affection as she held the hot body of her niece close, the soft downy hair tickling her neck as she cuddled her.

A poor substitute for a mother.

CHAPTER EIGHT

SEEING her empty pillow, Rico's first reaction was to panic, but he forced himself to lie there for a moment, ears straining to hear her voice, waiting for the bathroom door to open, for Catherine to come back to him. Running a hand along the bed confirmed what he knew. The uneasy sleep, the vague discomfort he had awoken with, were all explained as he felt the cool sheets.

He had been sleeping alone.

Deliberately he moved slowly, taking his time to shower, to dress, resisting the urge to find her, to demand to know where she was hiding.

Opening the nursery door, he stepped inside, staring for a moment at the two new ladies in his life. Lily was comfortable and contented, sleeping the innocent sleep of babies, with nothing more on her mind than where her next feed would come from. For a second his stern features melted, but it wasn't Lily's beauty that held his gaze, instead it was Catherine.

Rico frowned in concern. Her face was so pale, her posture awkward in the hard chair, and though his stomach still churned from their row last night, though his mind was still buzzing from her spiteful words, in the grey morning shadows the woman who had taunted him last night seemed but a distant memory. She was almost as childlike as Lily in her innocence—dark hair tumbling around her shoulders, the bulky rings on her finger looking out of place on such slender hands.

Moving quietly, he picked up the slumbering Lily, placing her gently in the crib and covering her before turning his attention back to his reluctant wife. Her eyes flicked open, and he watched as she accustomed herself once again to her new surroundings.

'So this is where you have been hiding.'

'Lily woke—' Catherine started, casting her eyes anxiously around the room, and Rico registered her fear and moved to reassure her.

'She's back in her cot.'

Catherine let out a low sigh of relief. 'I thought I'd dropped her.'

'Don't be silly.'

She was massaging her neck, stretching her spine, like an oriental cat awakening. One hand was raised behind her head, causing her gown to open just a fraction, allowing a glimpse of creamy bosom. Rico felt the breath still in his lungs. The child was gone now, the woman was back, and his features quilted. He straightened his back as his resolve returned and with a supreme effort he forced his attention away, focused instead on the sleeping baby.

'Are you going to work?'

It was a silly question really, for he stood in a dark suit, a heavy cotton shirt enhancing his dark complexion, a tie expertly knotted. Everything about him screamed wealth and success. His cufflinks caught the morning rays as he pulled the bunny rug higher around Lily's shoulders. 'I just came to give her a kiss before I leave. I will be home around seven this evening, ask Jessica to save her bath for me.'

Catherine gave a vague nod, staring fixedly at the wall in front of her as Rico tenderly kissed the sleeping babe.

'What will you do with yourself today?' Rico asked, straightening up but still refusing to look at her, and Catherine gave a brief unnoticed shrug, rocking idly in the chair and wishing this uncomfortable meeting was over.

'We might go for a walk, I suppose—do some shopping.'

'Here.' He handed her a wad of cash which Catherine didn't accept.

'When I said shopping, Rico, I meant for an ice cream or something. I'm sure even I can stretch to that.'

'Don't be ridiculous, Catherine. I'll arrange for some cards to be made up in your name, but for now you'll have to use cash.'

Still she refused. 'I've got my own money, Rico.'

'So what was that little lecture about last night?' Rico asked shrewdly, watching as the colour returned to her cheeks. 'I thought you said you were a Mancini now?'

'Mrs Mancini—you haven't been in here all night, I hope?' Jessica gave a worried frown as she bustled in, and heeding Rico's words about trusting the staff Catherine shook her head.

'Of course not. I thought I heard something and I was just checking she was okay. Rico wanted to give her a kiss before he went to work.'

'I'll be off, then.' He moved to go, but changed his mind midway. Turning, he fixed her with a black smile and walked over, ignoring the furious warning signs blazing from Catherine's eyes.

'Goodbye, darling.'

God, he deserved an Oscar.

Jessica, clearly used to being ignored, stood politely as he pulled Catherine into his arms, buried his face in hers and kissed her way too thoroughly. Mindful of her unbrushed teeth, burning with embarrassment at their audience, she stood stiff and unyielding in his arms. But Rico didn't seem to mind a bit. His tongue probed her lips, his hand lazily working its way under her hair, fingers massaging her tense neck. She could feel the cool metal of his watch, smell the fresh crisp scent of him, and as he pulled away Catherine changed her mind—it was she who deserved the Oscar, for it had taken every ounce of will power to keep from kissing him back.

'Bye, then.' That triumphant glint was back in his eye. *He's enjoying this,* Catherine thought darkly. *Enjoying my utter humiliation, enjoying watching me squirm. Well, two can play at that game!*

'Sweetheart?' Her voice was pure honey and she saw him frown quizzically as he turned back from the door, clearly bemused at the change in her. 'You said something about leaving me some money...'

She watched his face darken, but her smile stayed fixed and she held out her hand as he handed over the cash, a malicious glint in her eye to mask the tears.

'Hurry home, Rico.'

CHAPTER NINE

IT SHOULD have been perfect.

Day after lonely day she reminded herself of the fact.

A beautiful home, Lily growing more divine by the second, a husband she loved, everything there for the taking.

So why did she feel like a prisoner?

It looked good on paper.

Rico had already given her the answer, Catherine realised. On paper she had everything, but it counted for nothing. Hovering behind the curtains, watching the endless camera lenses still mercilessly trained on the house, she was scarcely able to believe that after two weeks public interest hadn't waned.

But then why would it? Catherine thought with a wry smile. She was as guilty as anyone of devouring the glossies, and the Mancinis certainly made for a good centre spread; the upcoming legal battle, and Antonia, grim and determined, giving endless interviews which Rico read without comment then promptly deposited in the bin.

Naturally, after he'd left for work, Catherine retrieved them.

She was desperate for some insight, frantically trying to join together the jumble of dots that made up Rico. Her heart just melted at the sight of a photo of him, dark and brooding, climbing into his car, his lips set in a grim line, eyes hidden behind dark glasses, the proverbial no comment all he had to say on the matter.

All he had to say full stop.

Since their first night back at the house enemy lines had been drawn, and night after lonely night she chided herself for her part in it. Day after day Catherine berated herself for her handling of things. Time and again she attempted to talk to him, to somehow fashion a path out of the stalemate they'd locked themselves into.

Time and again he pushed her away.

'Lily's grandparents are at the front door.' Jessica's nervous voice broke into her thoughts. 'I didn't know if I should let them in or not.'

Her first instinct was to say no, to let the staff sort it out, even to ring Rico and ask him what she should do. But Catherine reminded herself she was made of sterner stuff than that, and perhaps if she was ever to make an informed opinion she should listen to what they had to say—stop relying on magazines and find out the real story.

'Show them through.'

The sight that confronted her was one she hadn't expected. Bracing herself for the garish, overdressed woman she had seen at the funeral, she was somewhat shocked to see Antonia Mancini dressed in casual trousers and a pale jumper. Her make-up was minimal and her smile seemed genuine.

'Catherine.' She swept across the room in a moment and pulled her into an embrace as Catherine stood awkward and unsure. 'I'm sorry—too tactile for my own good sometimes. I'm just so pleased that you let us in.'

'I don't want to keep Lily from her family.' Catherine

smiled at the baby on the floor as Carlos and Antonia knelt down beside her and tickled her toes. 'Tactile' wasn't the word that sprung to mind after Rico's stern description of Antonia, but the effusive woman playing with Lily now seemed a world away from the person who had greeted her with such distaste at the funeral.

'She's beautiful, isn't she?' Antonia was positively crooning, and she flashed an embarrassed smile as Catherine stood there rigid.

Picking up the infant, Antonia waited patiently as Carlos sat himself down and then held his hands out, and nothing Rico could say would ever convince Catherine that the love that blazed in the elderly man's eyes as he took his granddaughter wasn't genuine.

'I think I've got a competitor for Carlos's affections.' Antonia smiled. 'Can I see the nursery?'

It was an obvious request, Catherine told herself, the sort of thing any doting grandparent would ask, and after only a brief hesitation she nodded. But Lily's grizzles halted the women at the door.

'Here.' Handing Carlos a book of nursery rhymes, she gave an embarrassed smile. 'She's due a bottle, but I've found if I read a few of these to her I can generally hold her off for a little while.'

Carlos took the book and eyed it distastefully before depositing it beside him on the couch.

'We will manage.'

'Of course.' Catherine frowned, taken aback by the abruptness of his gesture when she had only been trying to help.

'Carlos will be fine,' Antonia soothed as they made their way up the stairs. 'No doubt he'll be singing some

Sicilian lullaby to her by the time we go back down. He's been so looking forward to seeing her. Me too,' Antonia added as they walked into the nursery. 'I love babies—girls especially.'

'Did you have any? I mean…' Catherine was flustered. 'Do you have any children of your own?'

Antonia shook her head. 'My first husband and I weren't blessed, unfortunately. When Carlos and I married I thought…' Her voice trailed off for a moment, and there was a wistful gleam in her eye as she looked around the nursery. Her hands lingered a moment on the heavy wooden cot, and she stared at the picture of Janey and Marco Catherine had placed on a small table by the night-light. 'I was naïve, I suppose. I assumed I could step right in and take over, but Bella Mancini was rather a hard act to follow—at least in her children's eyes.'

'It must have been hard for you,' Catherine ventured, her mind working nineteen to the dozen. She didn't want to be taken in, but as she sat down in the rocking chair and listened as Antonia told her tale she found herself slowly warming to the older woman.

'It was,' Antonia agreed. 'Oh, not that I'm complaining. Carlos was marvellous, and once Marco went to…' She gave a helpless shrug and Catherine jumped in.

'Why did you send Marco to boarding school?' It sounded like an accusation, but Catherine deliberately didn't apologise watching Antonia's reaction closely, determined to hear the facts, to make up her own mind.

'Marco was out of control.' Antonia's eyes fixed on hers. 'Bella, their mother, had let them run wild—she was a working mum.' Watching Catherine's shoulders stiffen slightly, Antonia changed tack. 'I'm not against working mums, you understand, but Bella spent her whole time in the office and made up for it with her chequebook. Anything the children wanted they had—except their mother. Rico was an insular young man; there was no reaching him. He was eighteen years old by the time Carlos and I got married. Oh, I tried to get close. But—well, I'm sure I don't have to explain to you how guarded he is...'

She didn't. 'Guarded' certainly was an apt description, and trying to picture Rico as a young man was an almost impossible feat. He seemed born mature.

'As for Marco, he was heading for trouble—twelve years old and with no authority figure. Carlos adored him, but he was never very good at saying no to him. I thought if he went to boarding school, got some sense of worth instilled in him, discipline...'

Antonia was fishing for her hanky now, only this time her tears seemed real. Catherine suddenly felt sorry for her—there really were two sides to every story.

'Maybe I did make a mistake, maybe I should have hung in there a bit longer, but at the time...' She picked up the photo, staring at it for an age before softly replacing it. 'I was hoping to do things better with Lily—show Carlos and Rico that I can be a good mother and maybe somehow make things up to Marco. I know Rico will not be pleased you let us in, but I want to thank you, Catherine—thank you for letting Carlos and I have some time with Lily.'

'You're welcome.' Catherine went to stand, but the room suddenly seemed to be shrinking. Antonia's eyes bored into her as she held firmly onto the cot rail, steadying herself against a sudden overwhelming nausea.

'My dear, are you all right?' Antonia asked, pushing Catherine gently back down in the seat. 'You look ever so pale.'

'I'm fine,' Catherine croaked, and then righted herself.

'I'm fine,' she said again, only this time more forcibly. 'Just a bit tired.'

'You must be exhausted.' Antonia picked up her bag and as Catherine again went to stand she gestured for her to sit. 'I can see myself out, Catherine; you just sit there and rest a while.'

'I'm fine,' Catherine insisted, suddenly feeling foolish.

'You're worn out, my dear.' Antonia patted her shoulder in an almost motherly gesture. 'And undoubtedly you've got a lot on your mind.'

That was the understatement of the millennium.

Left alone, Catherine creased her forehead in concern, her hands fluttering to her stomach. The eternal calculator women reverted to sprang into action as she tried to remember a landmark—she'd been at work—no, shopping—the twenty-second... Her fingers drummed on the side of the rocking chair as she did the maths, trying to ignore the gnawing possibility that seemed to be gaining momentum, trying to push away a truth that couldn't be ignored no matter how she might want to.

How long she sat there she wasn't quite sure. But Jessica had long since taken Lily for a walk, and late-afternoon shadows had long since started creeping in when, chilled to the core, Catherine took herself to her room and lay on the lonely marital bed like a wounded animal, trying to fathom Rico's reaction when she told him.

Trying to fathom her own reaction to the news that was only now starting to hit home.

Her marriage was now for ever.

CHAPTER TEN

'I THOUGHT one actually had to give birth to suffer from postnatal depression!'

Flinging open the curtains, Rico looked down at her, and Catherine stared back, unblinking, watching his cat-like elegance as he started to prowl the room. He threw open the wardrobe and pulled out one of the many expensive dresses that had miraculously appeared. 'Or don't tell me—you're tired again!'

He had a point. Much as it galled her to admit it, Rico had every right to be scathing. Since Antonia's visit most of her days had been spent in the bedroom, trying and failing to work out some sort of plan, trying and failing to summon up the courage to tell Rico what was really on her mind.

But it wasn't just Rico's reaction troubling Catherine, it was her own take on things that terrified her the most. How could she even begin to contemplate having another baby when she'd barely adjusted to having Lily? How could a heart that already seemed stretched to capacity falling in love with one, fall in love with two?

'I'm bored, Rico.' Sitting up on the crumpled bed, Catherine refused to look him in the eye, woefully aware of her rather shabby appearance compared to his—the unkempt hair, the dark bags under her eyes, the shiny unmade-up face.

'Well, why aren't you at the park with Lily?' Rico protested. 'It's a beautiful day.'

'It's been a beautiful day since eight a.m.,' Catherine said with an edge to her voice. 'And I've been to the park—twice. I've been for a coffee at the bakery you told me about, and I've even been to children's storytime at the library—much to Jessica's horror. We're both falling over ourselves to find something to do.' When he didn't respond Catherine pushed harder. 'I want to go back to work, Rico.'

'You are *not* working.'

'I'm going out of my mind.' Catherine attempted to run a hand through her hair, but to her eternal shame—and Rico's rather obvious contempt—a knot midway prevented her.

'You could try going to the hairdresser's,' Rico responded nastily. 'Try making a bit more of an effort with yourself.'

His words stung. Catherine was painfully aware she had let herself go over the past couple of weeks, but with Rico leaving at the crack of dawn, only to reappear late evening, it was hard to summon up the enthusiasm to look gorgeous. Invariably he'd arrive home and roll up his sleeves, lavish attention on a receptive Lily, then disappear into his study. She could be dressed in a sack for all the attention he gave her, and now he had the audacity to stroll in unannounced at five p.m. and demand a sleek sophisticate purring on the couch and eagerly anticipating her master's return.

Well, she damn well wasn't going to jump.

'I'm not cut out for this, Rico.' She kept her voice even, tried to keep the note of urgency away. 'I've always worked, the same as you, and I enjoyed my career. Imagine if you suddenly had to give it up. Imagine if you were left alone in this house all day.'

'You're not alone, though,' Rico pointed out. 'You've got Lily.'

'I know that.' Catherine whistled through gritted teeth. 'But I truly think I'd be a better mother if I could work—even part-time.'

'Because we really need the money?'

His sarcasm wasn't helping.

'Because I really need something else.'

'No, Catherine.' He shook his head fiercely. 'This is a pathetic attempt to show me you're not after me for my money—a half-hearted attempt to show me you actually liked your life.'

'I did like my life.' She was shouting now, as she confronted this impossible man. 'I liked it a damn sight more than I like it now. I'm tired of being waited on, tired of staff hovering and attending to my every whim, tired of rattling around a massive house all day with nothing to do. I want to work, Rico, I want to cook my own meals now and then or ring for a pizza if I feel like it...' she shook her head in sheer frustration at his non-comprehending expression, desperate for him to understand. 'Rico, I just want to get used to my new family in my own way, to try and feel like a normal wife and mother.' For a tiny slice of time she seemed to reach him, registered something in his eyes that bordered on understanding, and she stood trembling for a moment, willing herself to continue, to bring things out into the open. 'I know what's worrying you, Rico. I know what you're scared of and I promise you that if I did go back to work then I wouldn't be like your mother.'

For an age there was silence. Catherine scarcely recognised the dark stranger staring back at her. 'That goes without saying.' His voice was a snarl. 'Because at least my mother knew how to treat her husband. My mother managed to make an effort. But tell me, where does my mother come into this, Catherine? What crap have you been listening to now?'

'There's no need to swear.'

'Oh, there's every need,' Rico snarled. 'You bury your head in magazines, you insist on having Antonia over, despite my express orders...'

She jumped back slightly, eyes widening as she realised Rico knew.

'You think I don't know that Antonia has been here? You think I don't know that you have let her in this house?'

'She's Lily's grandmother.'

'She's my father's *putana*. Nothing more, nothing less.'

His anger was palpable, a simmering rage that might explode at any moment, but Catherine was past caring. She had to get through to him—couldn't carry on this sham of a marriage. And even though Rico had crossed that line, the boundary that normally kept their rows decent, and opened the borders to a place Catherine wasn't sure she was ready to explore, she knew now was the time—knew there had to be changes if ever they were to move ahead.

'I want to go back to work, Rico.' Catherine's voice was firm. 'I'd still be here for you and Lily.'

'You're not here for me, though, are you?' His words

were like pistol-shots. 'You haven't been a wife to me since that ring was put on your finger. And you're certainly not here for Lily. You're lying up here, mooching around and feeling sorry for yourself. I've tried—my God, I've tried—to give you space. I've tried to understand you're grieving for your sister, and the wrench all this has been, but you don't make things easy.'

'Antonia said that your mother—'

'Don't mention her name in the same breath as my mother,' Rico roared. 'I can just imagine what Antonia said—just imagine the lies she's been feeding you when you've let her in. You'd rather believe her than your husband? You are my wife, Catherine, and you're going to start acting like one. You will go and have a shower, do your hair, and tonight we will go out.'

'No.' Her response was instant. Going out was the last thing she wanted to do tonight. 'Please, Rico, I really don't feel well.'

Instantly his expression changed, his anger evaporating, his face a picture of concern. 'What is wrong?'

'I just…' She hesitated a fraction too long, and Rico's grip tightened around her wrist as she tried to walk away.

'Just what, Catherine? Come on—you will tell me. If you are sick I will call a doctor.'

She almost laughed—almost, but not quite. A doctor was the last thing she wanted or needed right now. A simple kit from the chemist would be more appropriate. Oh, God… A bubble of panic welled inside her as she imagined his face if she told him the truth.

Imagined his features hardening as she confirmed what he had suspected all along—that she had set out to trap him.

'I don't need a doctor.' Shrugging his hands away, she headed for the bathroom.

'But if you are ill...'

'I'm not *ill*, Rico. I just...'

'Your period?' It seemed strange for someone so overtly chauvinist to say the word so easily; she had expected a rather more vague attempt—but then Rico was making great strides in being a New Age guy at the moment, rolling up his sleeves each evening and bathing Lily with an enthusiasm Catherine wished she could muster.

Turning, she gave a wan smile. 'It's due; that's why I was having a lie-down, I just didn't feel so good.'

'I'm sorry.' There was an expression she couldn't read in his eyes, a certain woodenness in his movements as he gave a small smile. 'I should have been more considerate, I guess...'

'It's no big deal.' Catherine's smile was equally false. 'I'm probably being a bit precious.'

'Catherine, if there is something you need to tell me...'

'There isn't.' Tears were brimming now and she blinked them back, but not quickly enough for Rico's shrewd glare.

'When you say it's due, what exactly do you mean?'

'That it's due.'

'When?'

She swallowed hard, scared to tell him but too terrified to keep it in. 'A few days ago.' In an effort to stop her tears Catherine's nose started to run, and a rather ungracious sniff was the only follow-up to her words. She couldn't bear to look at him—couldn't stand to see the knowing look in his eyes, the confirmation, if ever he'd needed it, that she had trapped him.

'So you could be pregnant?'

'I don't know.' Deliberately she kept her voice light. 'I'm a few days late, and given all that's happened—'

'You must see a doctor.'

Catherine shook her head. 'It's too soon—too early…'

'No!' Still she couldn't read his mood. His face was pale, but his gestures were decisive. Picking up the dress he had earlier discarded, he handed it to her. 'I will telephone the surgery now and have the staff bring the car around. We need to know, Catherine.'

He didn't wait for her response, assuming as he always did that Catherine would oblige, and left her standing as he marched out of the room. But Rico was right, Catherine admitted as she showered and quickly dressed. They did need to know. They needed to know where they stood— needed to work things out once and for all.

It was their first outing together since the funeral, and the mood in the car was just as lively. Time and again she opened her mouth to speak, to ask Rico about his take on this, but nerves overtook and she shrank back in her seat, staring instead at the parched gardens and trying to fathom her own feelings on the situation.

A baby was the last thing they needed. She knew that— knew their relationship, if you could call it that, was tenuous to say the least. And yet…

Glancing sideways, she took in his profile, her breath catching as it always did at the mere sight of him. It was so easy to remember being held by him, so easy to remember how he had adored her, the delicious place he had taken her to with his skilful lovemaking. That night was etched in her mind indelibly, but it took on more meaning now, and she dragged her eyes away from Rico, staring down at her stomach and trying to imagine a life within, her stomach swelling, ripe with Rico's child. As mistimed as it was, as calculating as he might deem it, inexplicably it excited her.

'We're here.'

Waiting for the driver to open the door, she could scarcely catch her breath, and her legs were like jelly as she stepped out of the car. Clutching Rico's hand, she walked into a large house, and it was nothing like any doctor's surgery Catherine had ever seen. But this was Rico's world, she reminded herself. No crowded waiting rooms for him. No thumbing through ten-year-old magazines or catching a cold from your fellow patients. Instead they were whisked through to an office, where they sat in massive leather seats behind a huge mahogany desk and a doctor introduced himself—a doctor who was as assured and confident as Rico, and, Catherine noted with relief, who didn't appear to be intimidated by him.

'Rico, it is good to see you!' Malcolm Sellers shook hands, smiling at Catherine as he did so. 'And this must be your lovely new wife.' He sat down. 'I was actually about to call you, Rico. Have the police been in touch with you, Catherine?'

Frowning, she shook her head. 'I haven't been home since the funeral—but why would they…?'

'Why have you been calling, Malcolm?' Rico's question was direct, and Catherine was grateful for it.

'The autopsy results are in.' He let the news sink in for a moment before carrying on. 'Naturally I don't have Janey's results, but with your permission, Catherine, I can ring and have them sent over, if you would like to go through them both together?'

'That is not what we're here for.' Rico's accent sounded more pronounced and, turning, Catherine saw his hands gripping the sides of the chair, his knuckles white under the strain. 'We are here for another matter entirely.'

'Even so,' Sellers pushed, 'it might be better for you both to go through the findings with me. There's going to be an inquest, and knowing the results prior to that might make things just a touch easier when hearing the whole thing played out in court.'

'We are not here to discuss our siblings, Malcolm. When we choose to do so will make an appointment.'

'If that's the way you want it.' Malcolm Sellers sounded resigned, and Catherine guessed he was all too used to Rico's stubbornness. 'But if you do have any questions then you know I'm always here. Now—' he forced a smile '—who's the patient?'

'Catherine,' Rico answered even as she opened her mouth to do so. 'We would like to arrange some tests.'

'What sort of tests?' Dr Sellers's eyes were on her, but again it was Rico who answered.

'A pregnancy test.'

'Rico.' Catherine smiled at Dr Sellers politely before turning to him. 'I can speak for myself.'

She couldn't be certain, but she was almost sure a dusting of colour crept up Rico's cheeks, and he snapped his mouth closed, reverting to the surly pre-adolescent manner he assumed when he didn't get his way.

'My period is late, Doctor.'

'And you're usually regular?'

It was Catherine flushing now, the boldness of before leaving her as she attempted to discuss her monthly cycle with this difficult audience. 'Well, I wouldn't set my watch by it,' she said quietly, scuffing at the floor with her foot. 'But I am definitely a few days late. Though I know it's probably too soon to tell.'

'Not these days.' Dr Sellers's voice was kind. 'Though I should warn you there can be a down side to finding out too soon.'

'Such as?' Rico asked, and Dr Sellers shot him a rather irritated look.

'Rico, I'm going to need to examine Catherine. Perhaps you could wait outside?'

Rico's eyes darted to Catherine's and he blinked a couple of times when she nodded.

'It might be better.'

Rico clearly wasn't used to being asked to leave, and Catherine half expected him to protest, but surprisingly he agreed, shrugging his shoulders in a curiously nonchalant gesture before strutting outside.

'Someone's getting a bit over-excited.' Dr Sellers smiled as the door closed none too gently behind him.

Catherine didn't respond. 'Furious' would be a more apt description. 'Trapped' might be another. Dragging her mind away from Rico, she concentrated on the issue in hand.

'You said there was a down side to finding out too soon. What is that?'

'A very long nine months, for one thing,' Dr Sellers said dryly, but then his expression turned more serious. 'This is a very fragile time in a pregnancy, Catherine. Sometimes I suggest that my patients come back in a week or two if nothing has happened.'

'I understand what you're saying, Doctor,' Catherine

answered, equally serious. 'But I don't really need the test to tell me I'm pregnant.'

She didn't. From the moment their stars had collided Catherine had felt different. From the second Rico had cruelly suggested the possibility it was as if she had known the outcome—had almost envisaged the moment in her mind. 'This is really just a formality.'

'So the test is for Rico's benefit?'

Catherine didn't answer. Instead she handed over her specimen bottle as Dr Sellers opened his drawer.

'I can't imagine he'd be one to settle for feminine intuition. Even as a teenager he questioned me on everything.'

'Rico?' Catherine was smiling now, enjoying the small talk, grateful not to have to listen to the ticking clock as her fate was decided. 'I can't imagine him as a sickly child.'

'He's never had a sick day in his life; it's taken all my powers of persuasion just to get him to have his cholesterol checked. Disgustingly normal, of course.' He gave a smile, glancing at his watch, then back to the tiny strip of blotting paper before him. 'No, I'm talking about when his mother died. Rico grilled me for hours, sure there must have been something I could have done, should have foreseen.'

'How did she die?'

For a second she thought he wasn't going to answer, but after a brief pause he gave a tight nod. 'She had a stroke. I'm not breaking any confidences by telling you—it was all over the papers, much like now. Rico wanted answers, and unfortunately there weren't many I could give him. No one could have foreseen it. It was especially hard for Rico. Carlos's English wasn't very good, and Marco was so much younger. It was Rico who had to deal with the press, the paperwork—Rico who dealt with it all, really.'

Tears were pricking her eyes now. This was another side of Rico she had never envisaged—a young man trying to do the right thing, terrified, but having to be strong.

'It's a shame he's not being so pedantic where his brother is concerned.' Doctor Sellers's voice forced Catherine's attention, and he caught her eyes and held them. 'I really think Rico should come and see me regarding Marco's results. As I said, Bella's death couldn't have been foreseen, but...' His voice trailed off and it was Catherine who filled in the gap, the hairs on the back of her neck suddenly standing to attention. There had been something in Dr Sellers's voice that unnerved her.

'What did the autopsy show?'

'Catherine, I'm sorry. I cannot discuss this any further with you. Marco was my patient; Rico is his family...'

She nodded her understanding. 'Do you know anything about Janey?'

Malcolm shook his head. 'I can ring through to your doctor, though—explain that you're seeing me now?'

Catherine thought for a moment. She liked Dr Sellers, liked his directness, the way he handled Rico, but despite her curiosity she actually understood where Rico was coming from. She needed some time to prepare herself, to brace herself before she heard about Janey's injuries.

Today simply wasn't the day.

'Can I have some time to think about it?'

'Take all the time you need.' Dr Sellers was pushing the test strip towards her now, watching her expression with knowing eyes. 'I'd suggest this is enough to be going on with for now. Are congratulations in order?'

She couldn't answer, her throat constricting, her stomach clenching as she eyed the test.

'Catherine, I do read the papers. I know a little of what you've been through, and if this result isn't what you were hoping for...' He gave a small cough. 'You are my patient, Catherine. Nothing that is said in this room goes further. You have been under a lot of stress, and as you know stress manifests itself in many ways. If you choose, then that can be what we tell Rico.'

'Thank you.' Her voice was a tiny whisper. 'And you're right. I'm not sure if this is the result I wanted.' She gave a small laugh, but it changed midway and came out as a sob. 'But deep down I knew it was the one I was going to get. I'll be all right, Doctor. There's no question of ending the pregnancy.' She went to stand, but Dr Sellers gestured for her to sit.

'In that case, I haven't finished with you yet. In fact, I've barely even started.'

CHAPTER ELEVEN

RICO was practically climbing the walls by the time she emerged, a good twenty minutes later, glassy-eyed, a touch pink around the cheeks, but relatively composed.

'What the hell took so long?'

'He wanted to examine me, take some blood—that type of thing.'

'You went for a pregnancy test, not a roadworthy test. Bloody doctors. Why can't they just do what you ask?'

'He did do as I asked.' She tried to summon more words, tried to carry on the conversation, but she simply couldn't do it.

'Well?'

'If you snap your fingers, Rico,' Catherine warned him, 'I swear I'll...' Her eyes lifted to his, the answer blazing there for all to see, and she saw his mouth open as he registered her hesitant face. She braced herself for some scathing response, waited for his scorn, but it never came.

'You're definitely pregnant?'

'I'm sorry if this isn't the news you wanted, Rico. Sorry—'

'Never, ever be sorry,' Rico broke in. 'Catherine, this is wonderful...'

'Is it?' She stared up at him, utterly bemused at his reaction. 'It's too much, Rico, too soon. You think you're happy now, but one day you'll throw it back at me, say that I—'

'Forget the past, Catherine,' he demanded, and how she wanted to—how she wanted to put it all behind her. But it simply wasn't that easy. Too much had been said for instant resolution. 'Whatever your motives, whatever the reason…'

'My motives?' An incredulous laugh shot out of her lips. 'Two minutes into this pregnancy, Rico, and you already throw it back at me…'

'What I'm trying to say…' He was silenced as a nurse walked past, and he shook his head proudly. 'This is not the place.'

He took her to a restaurant, one of those tiny dark buildings people wandered past unwittingly, a hidden gem in the middle of the city, and once inside led her to an alcove, waiting till she was seated before speaking.

'What I was trying to say—' Rico resumed the conversation as if they had only just left it '—is that this is not a conventional marriage.' His words were without malice, and Catherine nodded, glad they could acknowledge that truth at last, glad they were finally talking. 'Whatever has gone on in the past, surely now is the time to put it aside, to start afresh? We are having a baby, Catherine. Something good, something positive has come from our loss—why can't we just move forward?'

'Without even glancing back at the past?' Catherine questioned. 'I'm not like you, Rico. I can't just move ahead without a backward glance. You won't discuss your past; you won't even discuss what happened to Marco with the doctor…'

'Cannot today be just about us?' he asked. 'I know this marriage is for Lily, but surely…' He picked up her left hand, played with the heavy gold band for a moment before continuing. 'Can we make a fresh start, Catherine? Start this marriage over again?'

'For the baby's sake?'

Rico shook his head. 'For all our sakes. Catherine, I want you to be happy. I want us all to be happy. With commitment on both sides surely we can make it work? We have to make it work,' he finished, more urgently.

'I know we do, Rico,' Catherine agreed. 'Which is why I want to go back to work.' She watched his shoulders stiffen, but chose to ignore it. 'I'm struggling, Rico. Struggling to find my place in a world that's so unfamiliar. I need something more, need my friends around me now more than ever—and, yes, I admit that maybe I do somehow want to prove that I'm not totally dependent on you, but it isn't just about that. My work is important to me,' Catherine insisted softly.

'My mother hated working.' His admission startled her—not his words so much, but the fact he was for the first time volunteering information, and about his mother, no less. 'No one knew that. Even my father assumed she adored it, and I guess for a while she did. She started the family business,' Rico added proudly. 'One of only a handful of women who made it in the property business, at least in those days. She barely spoke English when she first came here.'

'She must have been very clever.'

'She had an amazing eye.' Rico shrugged. 'I have inherited it. I see an old property and it is as if I know how it should be. I don't have to consult books. It is as if my mind's eye can see it in its former glory. When we first arrived in Australia my parents scraped together enough money to buy an old townhouse in Carlton. My father was a labourer and under my mother's guidance they re-built it, and then they sold it. That was just the start. Soon my mother was hiring people, buying pockets of land for next to nothing. They are now worth millions. I think my first words were "bayside views". He gave a low laugh. 'That is a lie. I spoke only Italian till I was five.'

Catherine found herself smiling. 'What about Marco?'

'He was born here.' Rico shrugged. 'He was always an Aussie. I spoke to him in English, so by the time he went to school he could speak both.'

'So things were easier for him?'

Rico shook his head. 'I love my first language, Catherine; hell at school was a small price to pay. I can still remember being picked up from kindergarten and driving along the beach road looking for properties. They were good times.'

'She took you with her?' He heard the question in her voice.

'Antonia no doubt tells a different story,' he responded, ignoring her furious blush. 'But, yes, she took me with her—and later, when the business was bigger, when I was at school and my mother was working the same ridiculous hours I do now, she still came home every night; she still kissed us goodbye each morning.'

'So what went wrong?' Catherine pushed gently, seeing the wistful look in his eyes, and slamming her fingers between the shutters she just knew were about to come down.

'One day it became a job—not a labour of love, not a passion. Just a job. She had obligations—houses, cars, boats—and as you can imagine Antonia didn't come cheap.'

'Antonia?'

'My father was having an affair. He had barely worked a day in his life. It was my mother who provided for us and he got bored. That was my father's excuse anyway. The night before my mother died she had a headache. She was more tired than I've ever seen a person, and yet she still had to make calls, had to go and check out a property. I found her crying in the study. That was when I discovered she knew about my father's affair. She said she was tired, that she just wanted to lie down and sleep, that after the Christmas break she would sort things out... She died the next day. A stroke, the doctors said. It could have happened at any time. But I know different. If she hadn't been working hadn't been pushing herself—'

'You don't know that, Rico,' Catherine broke in, but she knew her words fell on deaf ears—knew there was no room for manoeuvre. But just when she thought it was over, just when she thought the conversation was closed, again Rico surprised her.

'Part-time, Catherine. You can work part-time if that's what you want.' His eyes implored her to listen. 'And the day it gets too much—the day you feel you shouldn't be there...'

'I'll stop.'

'You have nothing to prove to me, Catherine, but if this is something you feel you have to do...'

'It is.'

And now that he had given a little—now that he had allowed her to glimpse a tiny piece of him—perhaps for the first time since the police had arrived at her door Catherine allowed herself to relax, allowed herself to just sit back and take in the world around her.

Rico was amazingly good company. When he wasn't being superior, when he actually let up, he had a wicked sense of humour, and as the dessert plates were cleared away Catherine was amazed to hear that the laughter filling the tiny restaurant was coming from her.

'You should laugh more often,' Rico said, taking her hand. 'It suits you.'

'It feels good,' Catherine admitted.

'I want you to be happy, Catherine; I want us to be happy. You, me and Lily.'

'I want that too.'

On Rico's instructions the driver had long since gone, and they walked hand in hand along the Yarra River, following its majestic curves. The warm, still night air was filled with hope, and for a while they blended in—and Catherine had never been more happy to do so, never been more happy to seem two young lovers on the threshold of their future.

'Thank you.' She turned her gaze to his. 'For understanding.'

'Marriage is supposed to be about give and take,' Rico said lightly, but there was an edge to his voice. 'Hopefully I do a better job than my father.'

'Don't be too hard on him, Rico.' In the moonlight they stood, her eyes searching his, imploring him to listen. 'It must have been hard on him too. He was an immigrant, a labourer; I bet he was a proud, hard-working man.'

'He was,' Rico admitted, albeit reluctantly. 'Mind you, once my mother started making money he was only too happy to give up and reap the benefits of *her* hard work.'

'Are you sure he was happy?' There was a long silence, and Rico made to walk away, but Catherine pulled on his sleeve and after a slight hesitation he turned back, ready to listen to what she had to say. 'Normally it's the other way around—isn't it, Rico? Especially in Sicilian families. Normally the husband is the breadwinner; look at how opposed you are to me working.' He opened his mouth to argue, but Catherine was too quick for him. 'The man is supposed to be the provider while the wife stays at home?'

'Then why didn't he work? Why didn't he join her in the business, take over the books, do something to ease her load?' Rico countered, and Catherine hesitated before answering. Her answer was not one she was sure Rico was ready to hear.

'Your father can't read, Rico.'

'Don't be ridiculous.' Rico's laugh was derisive, the superior scathing man back now, but Catherine refused to be intimidated.

'I'm sure of it, Rico.'

'He's a clever man...'

'I'm sure he is,' Catherine responded. 'And a proud one too. Can you imagine how hard it must be for him, Rico? How hard not to be able to read his bills, the snappy little letters you send him? The small world he must live in when he can't even look at a newspaper?'

'You're sure?'

'I'm sure.' Catherine nodded. 'Please, Rico, try not to view him so harshly, try and understand your father's side too.' He gave a small nod which, however tentative, Catherine took as a sign of encouragement. 'Maybe it wasn't so easy for your dad to sit back and do nothing. However much I don't condone it, maybe in some way having an affair made him feel a man again. Who knows what goes on in people's lives, Rico? Only your mother and father know the full story.'

'And Antonia,' Rico added bitterly.

'Antonia knows your father's version,' Catherine said thoughtfully. 'And, however much you might loathe her, your father clearly loves her. Surely that must count for something?'

He didn't respond—Catherine had never really expected him to—but this time when he walked away he reached for her hand and took her with him, walking in pensive silence along the river. And despite the lack of conversation, despite the endless problems that lay between them, never had Catherine felt closer to him.

CHAPTER TWELVE

'YOU'LL be okay?'

Standing in the hallway, almost bristling with excitement at the day ahead, Catherine picked up her briefcase.

'I'll be fine.' She laughed. 'Yesterday was wonderful.'

'You were tired last night,' Rico pointed out. 'You fell asleep on the sofa after dinner.'

'It was my first day back,' Catherine answered, buttoning up her jacket and checking her reflection in the mirror.

She could scarcely believe the smiling face that stared back. Going back to work had truly been a godsend. With the eternal teacher shortage, her school principal had welcomed her back with open arms and Catherine had been only too pleased to run. Rico might not understand her need for independence, but even he had reluctantly agreed last night that she seemed happier. Oh, she wasn't stupid, knew that the money she would be earning would be like loose change to Rico, but it was *her* money, the independence she craved. It was a reason to put on her lipstick in the morning, a chance to use her brain, to escape the undoubtedly luxurious but nonetheless stuffy confines of the house. And even though it was early days she felt as if she now had so much more to give. Even though she had been physically tired, Catherine had been imbued with a curious high when she arrived home last night. She had played with Lily with the same gusto Rico managed to muster on his return, even woken to give her

her two a.m. feed. Going back to work was surely the right thing, and she moved quickly now to reassure Rico, terrified of having her new-found freedom taken away, determined to prove she could do it all. 'I've only got today to do, then I'm finished till next week; I'm hardly slaving away.'

'You realise you're in the newspaper?' He pulled the paper out of his briefcase and handed it to her, but Catherine shook her head.

'I don't need to see it, Rico. I know the journalists followed me to school yesterday, but they'll soon get bored; they'll soon find another family to hound.'

'It doesn't look good,' Rico insisted, but Catherine merely laughed.

'So the company shares are sliding because a Mancini woman is actually going out to work? We're in frantic financial trouble and relying on my part-time teacher's wage to support us? Come on, Rico, they're clutching at straws to make a story out of it—and anyway, it was your mother, a *mere* woman, who founded the company. Remind them of that when you blast them this morning.'

'You really don't give a damn what people think, do you?'

'Do you?' Catherine asked.

'Normally, no. But I am worried about what the social worker is going to say.'

'The social worker happens to be called Lucy,' Catherine said with a slightly weary edge. 'Lucy has two children herself, and if you'd bothered to find out you'd also know that her husband happens to be one of the leading consultants at the hospital. So she more than anyone understands that women need to work for so much more than money these days, Rico.'

'I never realised you were such a feminist!'

'Get used to it.' Catherine grinned. 'And if this so-called newspaper's article moves the sisterhood on an inch then I'll be a happy woman indeed.'

'Happy's good,' Rico said softly, and Catherine felt her smile fade, replaced instead with a nervous lick of her lips as their eyes locked. Tension seeped in, but not the head-on, angry confrontation that had become so much a part of them—this time it was a thrum of togetherness, a sexual awareness that had never really gone away, just faded a touch from neglect. And when Rico moved a step forward she shivered with excitement as he moved closer.

'Are you both off, then?' They both jumped as Jessica came out to the hallway, holding a bleary-eyed Lily, her hair all sticking up. Catherine felt her heart trip. The eyes staring back at her melted her for a second so fleeting, so fragile, Catherine was almost scared to acknowledge it—almost scared to comprehend that the maternal instinct the social worker had promised would ensue might actually be stirring.

Last night she had come home, tired but elated after her first day back at work, and as she had climbed the stone steps of her new home a curious bubble of elation had welled inside her—almost a need to get inside, to see the little girl she hadn't even realised she'd missed.

'I'll be back around five,' Catherine responded. 'Though I can't vouch for Rico.'

'Seven,' he quipped, but his face softened as he made his way over to Lily. 'So save her bath for me, Jessica. And as for you, little lady…' He tickled the baby's chin, and Catherine watched as her face lit up, a smile breaking on her sleepy face. 'Make sure Jessica chooses a good bedtime story for me to read to you—preferably one with no songs!'

'Is that what that awful droning was last night?'

He didn't answer, his face concentrating intently on Lily before he turned to Catherine with an incredulous smile. 'I think she's getting a tooth!'

'Really?' Making her way over, Catherine peered at the gummy mouth. Rico tickled Lily to ensure she laughed enough for a good view. 'She is too.'

Such was the happy atmosphere in the hallway Catherine was almost reluctant to leave it. For a while there they almost looked like a normal family, celebrating one of life's tiny milestones, and most amazingly of all she relished it. But Jessica was a stickler for the clock, and soon pointed out that if they didn't get a move on they'd both be late.

'I'll see you this evening.' Catherine smiled, kissing the plump cheek almost without thinking about it, taking in the soft baby smell and lingering just a second before turning away.

Now came the difficult part.

For the staff's sake, appearances were always kept, and every morning as Rico left for work they always kissed— only on this morning it didn't feel so staged; on this morning it felt like the most natural thing in the world. But though it might feel natural, it didn't lessen her awkwardness. A furious blush darkened her cheeks as she lifted her face to his, and something in the way his hand snaked around her waist, something in the way his lips dusted hers, held hers for just a moment too long, told Catherine this wasn't a kiss for the cameras. This kiss was loaded with the passion that had lingered unchecked for so long, loaded with the tenderness that was starting to tentatively grow between them.

'I'll see you tonight.' His voice was gruff, his pupils dilated as he stared down at her pink cheeks, taking in her glittering eyes, feeling her chest rise and fall against his. His head moved a fraction, so when he spoke his words were for her ears only. His hot breath tickled her ears, making her toes curl just at the sound of it. 'You can save your bath for me too.'

'No songs,' Catherine teased, but her eyes grew serious, the magnitude of tonight starting to take shape in her lust-dazed mind.

'No songs,' Rico said softly. 'But maybe we could put some music on, have dinner up in our room...' Reluctantly he let her go, but took her hand as they left the house, walking towards their cars. Rico's driver nodded and held the door open as Catherine dived into her rather less impressive, infinitely unreliable but much loved car, winding down the window as Rico knocked on it.

'I'm going to be late, Rico!' she warned.

'Will your feminist principles object to me buying you a decent car?'

'Not a bit.' Catherine grinned. 'You see, the wonderful thing about being a woman in the twenty-first century means you really can have it all. But nothing too flash,' she added hastily.

'Mustn't outshine the principal,' Rico said dryly, but his eyes were smiling. 'Here.' Tossing the newspaper through the window, he gave her one final knowing smile. 'You know you're dying to see yourself.'

'I couldn't be less interested,' Catherine lied, but she didn't hand the paper back.

'Suit yourself.' Rico shrugged, turning to go, then halting again. He swung around on a smart heel, a mischievous smile inching across his lips. 'And next time the press are around do up your blouse!'

Determined not to give him the satisfaction of knowing he'd piqued her curiosity, Catherine pointedly started her car and headed out of the long driveway into the peak hour traffic.

She didn't get very far.

Pulling into a side street, she almost tore the newspaper in her haste to get to the said article, scanning the photo with a critical eye and letting out a groan as she saw the rather vast expanse of cleavage, courtesy of a forgotten button. A loud toot had her practically jumping out of her skin, but her annoyed look faded into laughter as Rico's car slid past, with Rico giving a knowing wave as the headlights flashed.

Truly caught, there was nothing for her to do except smile and rather sheepishly wave back.

As she pulled off the handbrake, the smile stayed put.

Oh, it wasn't much—in the scheme of things it barely added up to anything—but sharing a laugh was always good: their history in the making, a tiny step in the right direction…

Her glow didn't last that long. Somewhere mid-afternoon, Catherine's elation at being back at work wore off. Her back ached and so did her head, with the children's raucous laughter growing more grating by the minute. Lily's two a.m. feed, was clearly catching up with her.

Even the thought of a night in Rico's arms barely lifted her gloom as she cleared up the classroom and pulled her bag over her shoulder. All she really wanted to do was get home and soak in a bath alone for an hour and sleep.

'It's good to have you back on board, Catherine.'

Marcus Regan caught her as she dashed out of the staff-room. With his glasses perched on the end of his nose, he was a typical principal in every sense, and though she dearly wanted to get home, Catherine adored her boss and would never dismiss him.

'It's good to be back, Marcus. I'm sorry it's only part-time, I know how short the school is.'

'We are at that.' Marcus scratched his grey hair and Catherine could see the worry lines on his kind face. She hadn't told him about her pregnancy—it was still early days yet—and wasn't looking forward to it, if the truth be known. Staff were scarce on the ground, and the way Marcus's voice had lit up when she'd rung to see if work was still available had spoken volumes. 'Some mornings I wonder if we're actually going to have any staff to run the school. Still, it's good to have you back, Catherine. How's married life treating you?'

'Wonderfully.' Catherine smiled. It was a lie she was so used to telling it came without thought, but remembering the way Rico had held her this morning, she was able to impart it with at least a semblance of honesty.

'Well, I'd better not keep you. We'll see you Monday morning.'

Lily was seriously getting more gorgeous by the day, and her little face lit up as Catherine dashed through the door. She held out her fat little arms for a cuddle, but the gush of tenderness that had filled Catherine on her return yesterday was markedly absent. Catherine literally felt as if she were going through the motions as she played with the little girl. Guilt tore at her heart, and she was eternally grateful when Rico appeared bang on seven to give Lily her customary bath. Catherine perched on the edge of the tub, watching with a quiet smile as the slick sophisticate disappeared before her eyes. She was almost tempted to invite the inevitable photographers outside to come in and witness Rico in tender mode. That superior face was softer now, his expensive silk tie ruined for evermore as it dangled in the soapy water, his five o'clock shadow dotted with bubbles as Lily splashed and squealed in delight, moaning in protest when Catherine finally declared the water was getting cold and Rico should lift her out.

'Now comes the hard part.' Rico held up Lily's sleepsuit, frowning as he wrestled two fat legs and two wriggling arms into the garment.

'Don't ask me to help with the buttons.' Catherine shuddered. 'No matter how hard I try to get it right, Jessica comes in and promptly re-does them.'

'Done,' Rico said proudly, handing her the now sleepy infant as Jessica appeared with a bottle.

'I warmed this for you.'

Taking the bottle, Catherine noticed that Jessica's usually shining scrubbed face was beautifully made up, and the smart shorts and blouse she usually wore had been replaced with a rather slinky little dress.

'You look nice.'

'Thank you.' A blush crept across her young face. 'Mr Mancini gave me the night off.'

'Oh.' Catherine forced a smile. How badly she wanted

to peel off her suit, dive in the shower and have some time to prepare for dinner. This was supposed to be a romantic night—what was the point in having a nanny if Rico was going to give her time off when they really needed to be together?

Left alone with Lily, Catherine held her, fed her, trying so hard to love her—but the familiar panic, heavily tinged with guilt, was gushing back now. She tried to push it away, tried to remember the tenderness she had felt only this morning, tried to recall the social worker's wise words.

Give it time.

But time wasn't on her side. Lily was here and now.

'She's asleep.' Rico crept in, picking up the sleeping babe and placing her tenderly in the cot before turning his attention to Catherine, his smiling fading as he registered her tense features. 'What's wrong?'

'Nothing,' Catherine lied. 'I'd better have a shower before dinner.'

'Dinner is down to us tonight,' Rico said easily. 'I gave the staff the night off.'

'All of them?' Catherine groaned, standing to her feet.

'All of them,' Rico confirmed. 'You said you wanted to be more *normal*, that you were sick of being waited on, wanted to do the normal things a wife and mother does, so I figured I'd give them the night off and it would make you happier. Come on, I'm starving.'

She'd asked for it, really. In fact, Rico probably thought he was being nice, was doing her a favour, but a weary sigh escaped her lips as she headed out of the nursery. Her back was really aching now, and the thought of peeling a load of potatoes just to feel normal frankly did nothing to raise her spirits.

Heading for the staircase, she frowned when Rico took her by the arm and led her to the bedroom.

'I thought you said you were starving?'

'I am,' Rico said mysteriously, opening the door and letting her walk in, watching in amused silence as she took in the rather poorly laid table and massive pizza box.

'Pizza?' A smile played on the edge of her lips.

'Rung for by yours truly.' Pulling a chair out, he sat her down before proceeding to cut her a rather too large slice. 'You said you wanted to be normal, needed some junk food—well, here it is.' After pouring some cola he helped himself to a slice. 'So, like I said, I've given all the staff the night off,' Rico explained further, 'and tonight we do what couples the world over do on a Thursday night when the wife is too tired to cook and the baby is finally asleep!'

It was the perfect solution—the perfect meal, actually—and enough to put a smile on her pinched face.

'I needed that.' Catherine smiled as Rico took the last slice. 'You've no idea how nice it is not to have to use a fork.'

'You certainly spoke more,' Rico commented. 'You still don't feel comfortable around the staff, do you?'

'They're nice and everything…' Catherine shrugged. 'I just find it hard to carry on a normal conversation with everyone hovering around me pretending not to listen.'

'They're not.' Rico grinned. 'I'm sure they've got better things to be thinking about than hanging on to our every word. They're probably bored to tears.'

Put like that, he almost had her convinced—but not

quite. Oh, she was sure the staff didn't find her riveting, but Rico had this magnetism, this aura around him, and Catherine simply couldn't imagine anyone being bored in his company. He filled her day, filled her nights—just the sound of his voice could change her mood, a smile from him could lift her spirits. But that was surely not what Rico wanted to hear right now.

'I really am going to have that shower now.' Standing deliberately, Catherine headed for the *en suite* bathroom, but Rico followed her.

'I just want you to be happy, Catherine.' Turning her to face him, he let his eyes meet and hold hers, and for some inexplicable reason she felt the sting of tears behind her eyelids. She wanted to be happy too—was sure she could be, if only Rico loved her. 'I don't want you to feel like a prisoner.'

'Hardly a prison.' Catherine gestured to the opulent room, but her smile wavered as Rico voiced what was clearly on his mind.

'Am I your jailer?'

She pondered his question. At any time she could walk away—she knew that deep down. And perhaps she could fight for Lily from her own corner—maybe with the right advice she could even win—but it wasn't Lily who kept her here, wasn't the child growing within her, wasn't the desire to give her niece a privileged lifestyle. It was Rico who held her within these walls. Rico her mind always drifted back to whenever it wandered—Rico who held her in the palm of his hand.

'Am I your jailer, Catherine?' he asked again, with an expression she couldn't quite read in his eyes. Only this time when she opened her mouth to speak he didn't wait to hear her answer. His lips came crushing down on hers, drowning out her answer, drowning out her own internal questions as she lost herself in his touch.

So much easier to feel his arms around her, to taste his cool tongue, to respond to his masterful touch to pretend for a while that maybe he did love her, than to deal with the impossible dilemmas that taunted her.

He undressed her in a moment, peeling away the suit easily, unclasping her bra, and she felt the groan of his approval as her breasts fell heavy and warm into his waiting hands. She wrestled with his clothes, and for that moment in time Catherine truly didn't care about the rhymes and reasons that had brought them to this point, didn't care she was his wife in name only. There was just a need, a simple primal need, to make love, to be made love to, to feel his naked skin on hers, to feel his arousal, to touch him as a lover, as a woman in a way she never had before.

She heard his gasp as her hands took the weight of his arousal. She marveled in the velvet steel of his manhood as she ran her fingers its length, closing her eyes in ecstasy as it snaked through her fingers—a jewel she had longed for, a jewel that tonight would finally be hers.

He took her softly at first, with kisses working over her neck as he slipped inside. Mindful of her condition, he kept his weight on his elbows, a delicious friction hovering on the outskirts, but then need took over, a natural desire so strong his soft strokes deepened. Like some heavenly feather, he massaged her most intimate depths, and her shivering climax dragged him in deeper until he exploded within her. Afterwards he held her in the matrimonial bed, as a husband should. His arms slid around her and there was nowhere to hide when his words cut the still dark air, the question that had hung over them repeated now, with infinite tenderness this time.

'Am I your jailer, Catherine?'

She pondered her answer a moment, her voice when it came so low Rico had to bring his face closer to catch her response.

'I'm here because I want to be, Rico—though I admit sometimes I wonder what it is I'm fighting for.'

'You are fighting for your family, Catherine,' Rico said softly. 'How we got here is irrelevant. We have to make the best of things.'

He probably thought he was helping, probably thought he was saying the right thing—but staring into the darkness, wrapped in arms she never wanted to leave. Catherine tried to blot out the awful inference behind his words, keep it all together just a little longer. Only when his breathing evened and she was sure he was asleep, did she give in—allowing salty tears that belonged to the night to slip into her hair as she awaited the refreshing sensibility of dawn.

CHAPTER THIRTEEN

'YOU have a phone call.'

Sitting up in bed, Catherine rubbed her eyes and desperately tried to come to. Surveying the room, the open pizza box, the clothes strewn everywhere, she knew it looked as if some sort of wild teenage party had taken place, and with her thumping head and Rico standing over her like some over-possessive parent as she took the call, the analogy only deepened.

'That was Marcus Regan—the principal,' Catherine explained, replacing the receiver and not quite meeting his eyes. Rico still stood there.

'I gathered that,' he quipped, clearly not impressed by the early-morning call. 'And I also gather you have agreed to go in to work this morning, despite the fact you swore this would be a part-time job.'

'It will still only be three days this week, Rico,' Catherine pointed out, pulling back the sheets and trying to feign a spring in her step as she crossed the bedroom, determined Rico wouldn't get a glimpse of just how awful she really felt. Marcus's phone call had caught her completely unawares, and had she had time to think, to register she wasn't feeling the best, she'd probably have refused his plea to come in and cover for a sick staff member. Right now all she wanted to do was crawl back into bed, pull the rumpled sheet back over her head and recall Rico's blissful lovemaking.

Or sleep; either would do.

'You look exhausted; you should be taking things easy…'

Catherine didn't answer, the toothbrush in her mouth not the best precursor to eloquence, but she let Rico rant for a moment or two before rinsing her mouth and smiling at his reflection, scarcely able to believe that the mere sight of him knotting his tie could have her stomach dancing.

'I'm five weeks pregnant, Rico, not eight months, and I think most women would think that I am taking it easy. I haven't even seen an iron since I moved in here, haven't so much as flicked on a kettle, so a day at work isn't going to kill me.'

'It's not you I'm worried about.'

He was flicking the end of his tie through the knot, concentrating as he tightened it, but his black surly mood was palpable.

Not for a second did he notice her paling face. His words were an instant slap to the cheek, and their intimacy popped like a child's soapy bubble in the warm afternoon air. Never before had she been brought down to earth more quickly. She felt as if she were falling, literally falling. The dizzy heights of their lovemaking had taken her to a dangerous place, a place where just for a second Catherine had felt as if she might fly, and now she was being put in her place. Rico, in his cruelly dismissive way, was reminding her exactly where her place was.

The intimacy, the tenderness, the closeness she had experienced had been only for the benefit of his child's mother.

'I have to go.' His voice seemed to be coming at her

from a distance, and when his lips grazed her cheek she yielded no response. She watched, watched from the mirror, as he checked his watch, then stalked into the bedroom and picked up his briefcase. 'I'll see you tonight.'

Somehow Catherine made it through the morning, but it was literally a case of going through the motions. Lily was kissed and farewelled, the traffic snarl as she approached the school negotiated, her colleagues greeted and her students faced. But it was as if she were operating on autopilot, every response made with barely a thought as her mind again wandered back to Rico, headed down that dangerous, forbidden path that constantly beckoned and which for a while she had been stupid enough to follow. Stupid enough to think that Rico Mancini cared for her not just as a surrogate mother to Lily, a solution to a problem and now incubator to the Mancini heir, but as a woman in her own right.

A woman who loved him.

The children seemed to sense her distracted mood, and their lively chatter grew more raucous. Never had Catherine been more grateful for the lunchtime bell, fleeing to the bathroom where she leant her burning face against the mirror as she recalled their lovemaking last night, sordid now instead of beautiful. In one cruel sentence he had reduced her to a tart, a woman who could please him at his will, provide for his needs, but never, ever get close.

She had only just made it to the bathroom in time. Her retching mingled with her tears, humiliation mingled with a pain that suddenly intensified. But not a sharp pain that brought release, just a dull, throbbing pain, familiar to women worldwide—the monthly price of femininity. But

there was no comfort in regularity, no comfort in the familiar feeling her body was imparting, just a horrible thud
of clarity. The back pain, the sinking mood of the past
twenty-four hours, the brink of tears—all a totally normal
response she had chosen to ignore. Refusing to acknowledge, till the facts were indesputable that her pregnancy
was actually over.

'I'll do some blood tests.' Malcolm Sellers's voice was
efficient, but kind. 'I'm not going to examine you at this
stage, because if there is a chance you're still pregnant
that could only exacerbate things.'

'I've lost it, haven't I?' Catherine was sitting pale and
drawn at his desk, wishing she could rewind the past hour,
go back to the safety of being with child, the tiny ray of
light that had for a while shone, but instead she was sitting
in the doctor's surgery. Her taxi had barely been out of
the driveway, before the nurse had ushered her in. She
was in the Mancini world, Catherine reminded herself.
Things moved quickly here—no waiting rooms to mull
over the inevitable, no buffers, just straight to the horrible
point.

'I think that's what you should prepare yourself for.'
Malcolm nodded slowly. 'The fact you have pain, that you
no longer feel pregnant…'

His voice trailed off and Catherine found she was
frowning.

'I don't know that I actually *felt* pregnant before. Although…' Her eyes sparkled with tears and she accepted
the box of tissues Malcolm pushed towards her. 'I did
suddenly feel close to Lily, felt as if I was starting to get

the hang of things a bit. Could that have been just because I was pregnant?'

Malcolm gave her a sympathetic smile. 'I'm sure those feelings will all come again in good time, but a good dose of hormones generally helps things along. You mustn't forget the terrible strain you're under, Catherine; you've just lost your sister, you have a new marriage, new home…'

She knew Malcolm was trying to be kind, trying to say the right thing, but each and every one of the problems he had outlined she could deal with if only Rico loved her. She missed Janey, missed Janey so badly it hurt, but if only Rico was truly beside her she could bear it. Without his love even breathing seemed an effort.

'I'll get these bloods couriered to the lab, and as soon as I get the results I'll come and see you at home. For now I want you to go to bed and try to rest. If the pregnancy is still viable it's the best thing you can do. Have you told Rico yet?'

'I've tried. His secretary is trying to get hold of him for me; hopefully he'll call soon.'

'I'll get hold of him for you; doctors generally do better with proprietorial secretaries than wives.'

'Shouldn't I have a scan? Isn't there something you can give me to stop it?'

'It's too early for a scan, Catherine—and, no, there's no medicine I can give you at this stage of pregnancy. Normally it's just nature's way of letting go of something that simply wasn't meant to be.'

In true private doctor style he saw her to a taxi, but she barely registered his kindness. A strange numbness seemed to have seeped inside her veins and she stared stonily ahead until the taxi pulled into the drive. Her legs were shaky as she pulled out some notes to pay.

The door opened on her first knock, and she held her private tragedy tightly inside as she headed for the stairwell.

'Mrs Mancini, I wasn't expecting you home…' Jessica stepped forward, the smiling Lily in her arms an aching reminder of what she was losing. 'Actually I'm really pleased that you are; I was hoping we could talk.'

Jessica was following her up the stairs now, an annoying presence when Catherine ached for privacy. 'Jessica, now's really not a good time; I came back from work because I don't feel well.'

'Oh!' Jessica moved Lily to the other hip. 'It's just…'

Still Jessica followed her. They were at the bedroom door now, and Catherine's stomach was cramping painfully.

'Just what, Jessica?' Her words came out too harsh and Catherine instantly regretted them, but she simply didn't have the energy to take them back. She ached to lie on the bed, to close the door on the world, but still Jessica hovered.

'It can wait…' Jessica's voice trailed off, and the young girl swallowed uncomfortably. 'It doesn't matter, Mrs Mancini. I'll let you rest.'

She lay there in the vast lonely bed, trying to relax, trying to give her baby, if it was still there, its very last chance.

Something that wasn't meant to be.

Malcolm Sellers's words rang in her ears.

Everything around her seemed to be slipping away and she was powerless to stop it. This baby meant so much

to her—a spark of hope, a bond that would bind her to
the man she loved, something good and true and real to
cling to—and now, as sure as the night followed day, she
was losing it.

No!

From the ashes hope resurfaced, a tiny stirring of the
strong woman she was. She would fight this, fight till it
was over. Till someone actually told her that her child
was gone she would cling on for dear life, do everything
possible to protect the life within. Concentrating on keeping her breathing even, she ignored the cramping pain,
drifting away to a place that was gentle and kind, melting
into the solace she had glimpsed in Rico's arms.

Somehow amidst the ruins she found the haven of
sleep, her hands resting on her stomach, trying to hold her
child within, fitful dreams causing her to cry out. As if in
response she heard Rico's footsteps on the stairs, the bedroom door opening on his pale tense face. Dr Sellers
walked in behind him, and one look at the two men's
faces dashed her faintly flickering hopes there and then,
told her it had all been in vain.

'I'm sorry, Catherine.' Dr Sellers was sitting on the
bed, taking one of her pale hands in his. Her eyes darted
to Rico, trying somehow to gauge his reaction. But he
stared sternly ahead, his eyes fixedly avoiding hers, his
jaw set in stone, muscles quilting around his face and his
hands clenched by his sides as the verdict was delivered.
'Your hormone levels have dropped since I took your
blood last week. They're supposed to go up,' he added
gently, as Catherine shook her head against the pillow,
pulling her hand away and shielding her eyes with it, try-

ing to block out a world that seemed to relish the dirt it dished out to her.

'It's called a blighted ovum, which means that there was a pregnancy, but only fleetingly. Quite simply, it never progressed beyond the very early stages. As I said in my office, sometimes this is nature's way of letting go and, hard as it is, you have to remember that. It was simply not meant to be.'

Not meant to be.

He could have been talking about her and Rico.

A love that had surely been there, however fleetingly, but that quite simply couldn't grow—no matter how she wanted it to, how she nurtured it, needed it. A love that wasn't meant to be.

'This is no one's fault,' Dr Sellers continued, pulling her hand down and trying to look her in the eye, but as her eyes shot to Rico he turned to him also. 'Neither of you must blame yourselves or each other for what has happened.'

Wasted words.

One look at Rico and she knew she had lost him for ever. One look at his black coal-chip eyes staring stonily ahead and Catherine knew that quite simply it was over.

'It's not you I'm worried about.'

The recollection of his words taunted her now. The baby had been his priority and she had lost it for him had followed her heart, ignoring her aching, tired body, and gone to work. Rico would never, ever forgive her.

If ever he had despised her that paled into insignificance now, as Dr Sellers left them alone. Rico was a distant figure, standing resolute and unreachable by the bed, and Catherine ached for him to sit beside her, to take her in his arms and tell her it was all okay.

'Rico…' It was all she could manage, but he didn't respond to her lonely cry, just stared fixedly ahead.

Lily's cries filled the hall, and they seemed to pierce her soul, a painful reminder of all she had lost. Rico pulled a blanket from the wardrobe, laid it over her, and for a second so small it was barely there he held her gaze, his eyes laced with pain, confusion, fear, even, and she ached to comfort him, for him to comfort her, for them to hold each other and weep for what they had just lost.

But just as quickly as he'd met her gaze he pulled away, his voice harsh and austere, a world away from the tenderness they had shared last night. 'Try and sleep.'

'Please don't leave me.'

'I have to go to Lily.' Still he didn't look at her, his voice as cold and removed as if he were addressing a stranger.

'Jessica can take care of Lily for a moment.'

'Jessica is at the shops,' Rico responded briskly, but still Catherine persisted.

'What Dr Sellers said about blame…'

'You need to rest, Catherine.' A pounding on the front door was all the excuse Rico needed to walk out, but Catherine called him back.

'Rico, I need you here with me. Surely one of the staff can get the door…?'

'There are no staff.' Rico's voice was void of expression, and she'd have preferred the familiar fiery man than the empty shell that stared back at her. 'Apart from Jessica, I gave them the weekend off; we were attempting ''normal'' this weekend, remember?'

He didn't slam the door, but still she jumped when he closed it, listening to his footsteps on the stairs. The low, angry voices barely registered as she lay staring at the ceiling, hardly blinking when the bedroom door opened and Rico and Antonia stepped inside.

'Antonia says this can't wait.' Rico's voice was clipped. 'I explained you weren't feeling well, but she was insistent.'

'I'm sorry.' Antonia stood awkwardly at the edge of the bed. 'I thought Rico was making excuses when he said you were unwell, but clearly…' Her voice trailed off and she turned to go, but then changed her mind. 'I'm sorry for intruding. I had no idea Catherine was pregnant—no idea this was anything other than a marriage for appearances' sake. It would seem I misjudged you both.' Her hand reached out and she patted Catherine tenderly on the arm, 'I'm sorry to hear about your baby, Catherine.' Her eyes drifted uncomfortably to her stepson. 'I'm sorry for your loss too, Rico. I know it might seem hard to believe, but I do understand what you're going through.'

The look Rico gave her clearly indicated he assumed Antonia had absolutely no idea, but a wistful note in her voice stirred something within Catherine. 'You lost a baby too?'

Antonia nodded slowly. 'I lost four,' she replied slowly, fiddling awkwardly with her earrings as Catherine stared back. 'And each time I was told not to worry, that there were years ahead for me to have children, that this was just nature's way…' Her voice wavered for a moment before continuing. 'And I know how empty those words sound at the time, so I won't waste your time with them.'

'There was something you wanted to say?' Catherine offered as Antonia turned to leave.

'I'll come back in a few days,' Antonia replied. 'When you're feeling a bit better.'

'I'm fine.' Pulling herself up on the pillows, Catherine forced a brave smile. 'It really was very early days—I'm probably being a bit precious, lying here. If I hadn't known I was pregnant I would have just assumed it was...'

'It's not the physical pain, though, is it?' Antonia said wisely, and not for the first time Catherine found herself warming to her; not for the first time the enemy didn't seem quite so unapproachable.

'I'll leave you two to it,' Rico said uncomfortably, but Antonia called him back.

'You should stay, Rico. What I have to say affects you both.'

Still she stood stiff and awkward, but there was a dignity about her as she spoke, and Catherine listened with both interest and admiration as Antonia addressed her stepson.

'I was wrong to expect you to accept me all those years ago, Rico. I hurt your mother, and you had every right to hate me, but in my defence all I can say is that I did love your father very much. I still do.' Her words were soft and emotive but Rico stood unmoved.

'So money had nothing to do with it?' he asked mockingly, but surprisingly Antonia nodded.

'I liked the money too, Rico. I admit that. I also admit that I was wrong to accuse you of underselling the business. You gave your father and Marco a more than generous price. They weren't prepared to work and, as lucrative as the company was under your mother, it only really turned into the empire it now is once you took it over.'

'I know all that,' Rico said rudely. 'So why are you really here, Antonia? Why the supposed olive branch?'

'Rico!' Catherine broke in, appalled at his rudeness. 'At least hear what Antonia has to say! I'm sorry,' she said, flustered, turning to the older woman, but Rico hadn't finished yet.

'Don't apologise on my behalf, Catherine.' His eyes turned to his stepmother. 'I don't know what your agenda is this time, Antonia, and I don't know what your motives are for coming here. If I appear rude then so be it; I make no apology. I can take what you did to me, Antonia, but it's the hurt you've caused those closest to me I cannot accept, and I will not let you do it again. So I'm warning you, if you're going to say anything to upset my wife, now really isn't the time. I swear to God if you upset her tonight, when we've just lost our child, you'll never set foot in this house again and I'll do whatever I have to do to ensure you have no further contact with Lily.'

'I have no intention of upsetting Catherine.' Antonia stood resolute, but as she spoke her voice wavered, those well-made-up eyes brimming with tears that could never be manufactured. 'And as for Lily—I've instructed our solicitor to withdraw our application for custody.'

Someone gasped, and it took a moment for Catherine to realise it had been her. Her eyes darted to Rico, trying to read his expression, but he stood tense and silent, his jaw firmly set as Antonia tentatively continued.

'Carlos and I have spoken at length and we realise that Lily deserves more than two retirees can give her. As much as we love her, as much as we want to be there for her—well, with the best will in the world we're in our sixties…'

'So why the sudden change of heart?' Rico's voice told Catherine he remained unconvinced, eternally suspicious. Antonia's tears wouldn't move him an inch. 'You haven't aged a decade in the last few weeks. What made you suddenly decide to give it all away?'

'You did, Rico.' Antonia looked across at her stepson. 'You and Catherine have turned your worlds upside down to provide a home for Lily. Look, I admit that until now I thought this was nothing more than a marriage of convenience, nothing more than a sham to win round the judges…'

'And even then you were prepared to walk away?' A muscle was pounding in Rico's cheek and it seemed to match Catherine's own heart-rate as Antonia blindly continued.

'Even then.' Antonia nodded softly. 'It hit me how much you must love Lily, Rico. That you would give up your own chance of happiness, live in a loveless marriage to ensure your niece's future; you too, Catherine.' She turned and smiled, not noticing Catherine's face paling on the pillow, her hands clenched by her sides as the nails hammered deeper into the coffin. 'I know I couldn't do it.'

'You really love my father?' Rico's voice was raw.

'I've always loved your father, Rico,' Antonia replied softly, 'and I always will. I'm just sorry it caused so much pain for so many people. I don't expect your acceptance or forgiveness, Rico. I want it, of course, but I understand if it's too much to ask. What I do ask though, is that your father and I can have regular contact. We want to be a part of Lily's life, Rico—hopefully now for all the right reasons.'

Rico gave a small nod, his expression still wary, but his Adam's apple bobbed a couple of times before he spoke, and when it came his voice was laced with emotion.

'And you shall be.' For the first time he looked at Antonia without malice. For the first time his voice was soft when he addressed her. 'I will see you out.'

How long she lay there she wasn't sure, but darkness had replaced the late-evening sun, the shadows matching her heavy gloom. Lily's heavy sobs flicked into her consciousness and she held the pillow over her head, trying to block out the cries; the pain in her stomach was easing now, and Catherine missed it.

Missed the pain that matched the agony of an ending to what had never really begun, to tentative dreams that had never really stretched their wings.

She held her breath in her lungs as she heard Rico cross the landing, heard the nursery door close. Lily's cries gave way to silence and she waited, waited for him to come to her—if not to make things better, then to make things a little more bearable. But as the lonely moon drifted past her window Catherine knew she had lost so much more than just her baby tonight,

In the scheme of things she knew her loss barely registered a blip, that maybe Dr Sellers was right—yes, she was young; yes, there would be other babies. But she wanted that one, wanted the child she had lost this day, a baby she could almost see, almost feel. This was the baby she ached for, this was the baby she mourned, and if Rico wouldn't come to her now, in the depths of her grief, couldn't mourn the child they had just lost with her, then what was the point?

No point at all.

There were no ties that bound them now. No baby to unite them, no custody battle to pursue, just a mere legality that would be taken care of easily.

A marriage in name only that had been over before it had started.

She dressed in a moment, packing quickly. She hadn't been in Rico's world long enough to accumulate much, except perhaps the broken heart that would surely weigh her down for the rest of her days.

She wandered the lonely house, bracing herself at each door to witness his beauty—in the lounge, perhaps, nursing a whisky, or in the study, working long into the night. Finally she found him, asleep in the rocking chair, hiding from her as she had from him, Lily dozing in his arms.

Lily Mancini.

A smile ghosted across her face at the sight that greeted her.

How she couldn't have seen it she truly didn't comprehend. Lily could be Rico's child—the same long dark lashes swept over slanting cheekbones, the same full, slightly superior mouth, that even in sleep never really relaxed.

And she loved her.

Loved her enough to do the right thing by her.

To give her the life Janey would have wanted for her.

Slowly she ran her fingers over the soft down of the sleeping babe's hair, gazing now not at the child who slept but at the man who held her, meeting his stare as his eyes flicked open.

'I'm going, Rico.'

He stared back at her, taking a minute to focus, his bewildered expression deepening as he took in her clothes, the bag at the door and the utter defeat in her voice.

'Catherine—' He went to stand, but Lily let out a moan of protest and he moved quickly to gently hush her. He lowered her into the cot, soothing the babe with words as his eyes implored Catherine to hold on, to wait so they could talk. 'You can't just go.' Lily was starting to fret now, perhaps sensing the loaded atmosphere, but Rico was facing Catherine, demanding that she listen. 'You should be in bed. You're not well…' He gestured to the crying infant in a final stab at reaching her. 'Lily needs you.'

'No, Rico.' Catherine's voice was a hoarse whisper. 'I thought she needed me, I thought I was the right person to bring her up—convinced myself that was what Janey would have wanted. But Janey hated me. Why do I flatter myself that she'd want me raising her child?'

'Because you know this is the right thing to do!'

'Janey despised me, Rico.' Catherine's words were without pity, without bitterness. 'Janey wanted money and wealth, and she'd have wanted the same for her daughter I truly thought I was doing the right thing, truly believed that I could do a better job than Antonia.' She shook her head, bit hard on the tears that were now threatening, refusing to break down at this late stage, determined to escape with her last shred of dignity. 'Antonia loves her;

she proved that today. Lily's going to grow up surrounded by people who adore her.'

'She needs you,' Rico insisted, following her out to the hall. 'I need you.'

His words stilled her, but only for a moment. She squeezed her eyes closed as his words ricocheted through her, hating him for making this harder than it needed to be.

'You don't, though, Rico.' She couldn't bring herself to look at him, couldn't bring herself to turn around and witness what she was losing. 'You've won. As long as you allow Antonia and your father to see Lily, you can have her.'

'I need you,' he said again, his hand on her shoulder, turning her slowly around, but his strong features blurred through her tear-filled eyes.

'No, Rico,' Catherine said softly. 'We lost our baby tonight and still you didn't come to me. If you need me so much, why weren't you there?'

'There were reasons, Catherine, and if you will give me a moment I will explain them to you…'

'I'm tired of your excuses, Rico—tired of the *reasons* you conjure up to hide your heart from the world. So I'm going, Rico, because I can't live like this for a moment longer. I can't live in a marriage that isn't about love, and despite what you say, despite the contempt you regard it with, I still believe in love, still believe in the fairytale. Still believe that one day I will be loved as I deserve to be loved.'

'Then stay.' His words were ragged as he followed her to the stairwell, pulled at her jacket in a desperate attempt to stall her. 'Hear what I have to say before you walk out on us...' He grabbed at her handbag as she started to descend the stairs, urgency in his voice, haste in his actions as he tried to reach out to her.

'Rico, please.' She was pulling at her bag now, in a futile tug of war, tears blurring her vision, her head dizzy with emotion. She wrenched it away, the sudden jolt as he let go was all it took for her to lose her footing, and the banister was out of reach as her flailing arm reached for it.

'Catherine!' His shout was one of pure anguish, but his reflexes were like lightning. Instinctively he reached out and pulled her back from the brink, grabbing her into the safety of his embrace—the only thing that stopped her from toppling the dangerous length of the stairwell. As she looked up through startled eyes she registered the horror in his expression at her near fall, and their chests rose and fell in unison as the shock of what had nearly taken place dawned.

It was Rico who recovered first, his voice ragged, his breathing rapid, still holding her trembling body in his arms, still somehow protecting her even as he finally let her go.

'Is that how badly you want to leave, Catherine? That you would throw yourself down the stairs rather than stay and talk to me?'

She hadn't been throwing herself down the stairs, it would have been a simple accident, but she chose not to correct him. A metaphorical door was opening, and Catherine chose to go through it.

'I'll leave in an ambulance if that's what it takes, but I am going, Rico.'

'I'm not your jailer Catherine.' There was a curious

dignity in his voice as he stared down at her, a wounded pride in his manner now he had released her from his arms. 'This was never how it was supposed to be.'

'I know that,' she whispered through pale, trembling lips, then walked slowly down the stairwell, unhindered physically, but with every cell in her body begging her to stay, to return to all she loved. She turned to him with tear-filled eyes, trying to block out Lily's sobs but failing to do so. 'Tell Lily I do love her. I'll call.'

'When?'

She shook her head, too raw to contemplate a future when she could see Rico without breaking down, share in her niece's birthdays and milestones without dying a little inside for all she had lost.

'I don't know, Rico.' She stared up at him, this haughty, brooding man she had loved—yes, loved—from the second she had laid eyes on him. A difficult, complicated man who simply couldn't lower his guard, a man with a brilliant mind who couldn't get his head around something as simple as love, and the distance between them, the safety of the front door open in her hands gave her the strength to finally speak the truth. 'You were right to be suspicious of Antonia, Rico, and you were right about Janey. But you were so very wrong about me. I never wanted this house, Rico, never wanted the servants or the cars. I love you. The only thing I wanted out of this marriage was you, and it was the one thing you weren't prepared to give, the one thing that wasn't up for negotiation. Well, I can't do it—I can't live in a marriage that looks good on paper; I can't survive in a marriage without love.'

'Catherine, please!' He was bounding down the stairs

three and four at a time, taking the impressive stairwell in barely a stride, but she was too quick for him, slipping out of the heavy door like a thief in the night and then slamming it closed.

He didn't follow.

She'd never really expected him to.

It had all just been a game.

CHAPTER FOURTEEN

EXHAUSTION, grief, pain—they had no meaning now. It was as if she had somehow passed through a barrier and come out the other side, numb, almost without emotion, as if Rico had wrung every last drop out of her and left her with a curious void that must surely be her life now— an empty, dark abyss where her heart and her spirit used to reside.

She drove aimlessly, taking the beach road from the city and heading along the horseshoe of Port Phillip Bay, watching the still, inky water. The same moon that had drifted past her window was like a glitter ball above the water, and the stars danced around, inviting her to step out and take in their grandeur, but for a while she ignored the call, driving with more purpose. Her journey had meaning now, and she acknowledged the magnet that had drawn her here. The grief that had never really been explored was a festering wound that needed to be lanced if ever she were to find peace…

Pulling her car in amongst the tea trees, she gazed at the tombstones silhouetted in the moonlight, then wandered through the stony paths till she came to the soft mound of earth that was Janey's. The funeral flowers had long since died, but a fresh sprig lay on top, beautiful in its simplicity, and sinking to her knees she fingered the warm soil, ran her fingers along the petals of the flowers.

She pulled the card out and read it, and her heart seemed to split in two.

Sleep peacefully
We will do our best for Lily
Rico and Catherine.

The fact he had been there, that the detached, distant Rico had been to Janey's grave, blurred the edges of her reality. He had spoken on behalf of them both, signed her name, promising to do their best for a child left alone, and it tore at her very being.

The tears that had always been there were given permission to fall then, and she sobbed into the lonely darkness, her wails guttural, primitive as she wept for the beautiful sister she had lost, the sister taken too soon, wept for the parents she would always miss and for the baby she would never hold.

She cried for Rico too.

For the man who had danced in her dreams, who had allowed her to glimpse all he could be, if only for a fleeting time—the man who had held her, loved her, even if he couldn't admit it to himself.

A man she would mourn now for ever.

'Let it out, Catherine.'

For a second she stilled, frozen for a moment in time as Rico knelt beside her.

'Leave me,' she sobbed, but Rico as usual ignored her, instead wrapping his arms around her, pulling her into his embrace as she struggled like a cat. 'Leave me,' she pleaded again, but she felt him shake his head, and the vice of his grip was curiously comforting, something to hold onto as tears again took over.

'Let it out, Catherine,' he said again, and suddenly the whys didn't matter. Rico was here, and as she wept his arms were around her, holding her, almost an extension of her own body, a rock to lean on. And however temporary, however ill-fated their union, for a moment or two she allowed herself to cling to him, not strong enough to face this moment alone.

'Janey loved you.' He was trying to comfort her, trying to say the right thing, but his words only fuelled her pain, only widened the abyss of her loss.

'She hated me—how can I look after her daughter when she hated me?' Catherine gulped. 'It's time I faced the truth.'

'Is it?' His question forced her attention. Her shimmering eyes flicked up to his, and her sobs gave way to gentle hiccoughs as he stared back at her. 'Tonight I found out the truth, Catherine. Tonight I found out what really happened to Janey and Marco—that is why I didn't come to you. I truly thought you were too weak to hear it, that now wasn't the time.' He took a deep breath, and for a second so small it was barely there she swore she registered tears glistening in the dark pools of his eyes, swore that for once in his life emotion truly had the better of him. 'It wasn't easy to hear, Catherine, but it is something you need to know, whenever you are ready.'

Summoning strength, she stared bravely back at him. 'I'm ready.'

'Not here.' Standing, he pulled her up, led her out from the graveyard, across the deserted street. They wandered through the bracken till she felt the cool crunch of stones beneath her sandals. She gazed out at the water before sitting down on the cool ground and staring up at the stars. He wrapped his jacket around her, his eyes narrowing in concern as he felt her frozen pale cheeks.

'It is too cold here, Catherine. You are not well; you should be at home...' His voice trailed off, the word 'home' had been placed out of bounds by Catherine, and as much as it tore him he had to respect that.

'I can't go back, Rico.'

He nodded, staring at her for a moment, clearly desperate to take her in his arms, to tell her the truths that needed to come out, but her pallor concerned him.

'We could sit in the car; I could put the heater on.'

A tiny shift of her head told him he was wasting his breath.

'Wait there.'

She didn't respond, just stared into the twinkling sky as Rico wandered over the beach, gathering driftwood. Her tears had left her exhausted—spent, but curiously detached. It had been cathartic cleansing so deep she felt almost void of emotion now, as if nothing more could hurt her, nothing more could touch her.

He knelt close by, parting the stones and filling them with driftwood, lighting the leaves and fanning the tiny flames until the wood caught. And still she said nothing, just gazed into the firelight, mesmerised by its beauty. The hint of eucalyptus as the flames licked the heavy logs was comforting somehow, and the heat from the fire warmed her chilled bones as Rico sat beside her.

'They weren't drinking, Catherine.' His words were soft, but very measured. 'And they hadn't been taking any drugs. As I was seeing Antonia out Dr Sellers came back.

We both spoke to him; he took us through the post mortem results.'

'But Marco staggered out of the restaurant; the doorman said he was so drunk he could barely speak…'

'He had a stroke.'

A gasp escaped her lips, a strangled gasp and her hands shot down and held her cheeks. Her mouth opened and shallow breaths came out in a grief so raw, so painful she was sure the scream that resonated around her head must be audible.

'Marco had a stroke—that's why he lost control of the car, that's why everyone assumed he had been drinking. And the saddest part of it is they were actually out celebrating—celebrating the fact they were going to get their lives on track.'

'How do you know all this?'

'I spoke with Jessica; when she returned from the shops we had a long talk. I think she was waiting for me to ask.'

'She probably was,' Catherine admitted. 'She's been trying to talk to me about it, but I kept pushing her away.'

'You should have listened,' Rico scolded softly. 'We both should have listened. Janey loved you, Catherine. She told Jessica that you had both been right to say something, that you in particular had always been right, that she was living life too fast and too dangerously and it was time to slow down. She said she knew it was time to grow up, to take a leaf out of your book and face up to her responsibilities. She was proud of you, Catherine; she wanted to be like you. You should talk to Jessica also,' he added. 'I think it might help you.'

Catherine nodded, staring into the flickering fire for a pensive moment, then turning back to Rico as he carried on talking. 'Jessica gave me some home movies—videos they had taken...' He swallowed hard, his Adam's apple bobbing up and down, and she could feel his hesitation. His usual reserve was battling to take over, but he fought it, dragging his eyes back to her as if she was what he needed to continue. 'I prepared myself for the worst when I put them on—a drunken party, perhaps, Lily crying in a corner... I've no idea what I expected to see, but never in a million years could I have envisaged the love I witnessed.'

'Love?'

She was sure she must have misheard him, somehow misinterpreted the simple yet intricate word, but Rico nodded slowly, that beautiful full mouth wavering slightly as emotion betrayed his usually steady voice. 'They loved each other, Catherine. To anyone else it would have been the most boring home movie ever, but there they were, cooing not just over Lily, but each other. And, as blind as I might appear in matters of the heart, their love was obvious.'

'So why did she say those terrible things?' Catherine asked.

'Maybe it was safer for her to believe them?' Rico suggested gently, taking in the tiny frown that puckered her brow, those delicious brown eyes blinking at the brilliance of new perception. 'Maybe in that messed-up head of Janey's it was easier to convince herself she was in control of her own emotions? Maybe she loved Marco so much that she did trap him, did everything in her power to ensure he married her? I don't know all the answers, Catherine, but one look at the video and you will be convinced also.'

'We can play it for Lily.' Her words were a whisper as bittersweet relief flooded her veins, because something had finally been salvaged from the wreckage, because Lily would have some precious memories to cling to of parents who had, it seemed, loved her after all.

'*You* can play it for Lily,' Rico corrected softly. 'Catherine, I love Lily, but despite your doubts, despite how hard it has been for you, I know in my heart you are the best person for her. You will be a wonderful mother.' His hand dusted down over her stomach, held the hollow where there should have been their child, and it was Rico's tears she witnessed now, with pain, pride, agony etched in each proud tear that scraped the razor of his cheekbones. 'You would have been a wonderful mother to this one too.'

'I'm sorry, Rico. Maybe I did do too much. Maybe going back to work after all I'd been through was just—'

'Hush.' He placed a finger to her lips. 'Don't do that to yourself. I never blamed you, Catherine, not even for a moment,' he whispered. 'I blame myself.'

'But why?' Catherine begged, her mind in turmoil. Seeing Rico, usually so strong, so utterly self-righteous, plagued by doubt, seeing this proud, dignified man in such pain, tore at her very being. The pain they had unwittingly inflicted on each other was almost more than she could bear. 'How could it be your fault?'

'Because when I found out you were carrying my child I was pleased for all the wrong reasons. I wanted you to be pregnant, Catherine—wanted you to be having my child. Not because I wanted another baby, but because I wanted you! But seeing your pain, hearing Antonia talk, it hit me just what we had lost. Our baby, Catherine. Our child. It was only then I realised how much I'd wanted it too.'

And though she ached to comfort him, to say the right thing, her mind stalled on the middle of his heartfelt speech, the rest of the words a blur as those three little words hit home.

'You wanted me?' Her voice was incredulous and she quickly fought to check it—scared, so scared, of raising her hopes only to have them dashed again; sure, so sure, she must somehow have misheard him, misunderstood. But those dark eyes were staring back at her unwavering, with love blazing brighter than the fire that warmed them.

'I've always wanted you,' Rico said slowly. 'I've always needed you. You changed my world, Catherine, made me open my eyes and see things from your wonderful perspective. You see the good in people,' he explained gently. 'You hang on in there despite the punches and somehow you find the best in everyone—even me. Tonight, when you told me you loved me, I wanted so badly to tell you I loved you too—to take you in my arms and weep with you for our baby...'

'You got here in the end.' Catherine smiled bravely, but when he shook his head and the shutters came down again she felt her heart split in two.

'It is too late for us, Catherine.'

'No!' Her shout was instantaneous, a furious yet heartfelt reaction; to be so near, to have got so close only for him to pull back, was more than she could take.

'Don't you dare hold back on me now, Rico. Don't you dare give with one hand and then take with the other. How can you say you love me, you need me, and then just shut me out?'

'Because as you said before, Catherine, you should be loved as you deserve to be loved, and I cannot promise you that. My mother died young, my brother also. Dr Sellers wants me to have tests; he says it may be hereditary, that there is a chance it could happen to me also. I cannot put Lily through another loss, and I will not put you through it either. How can I stay when I don't know if I can promise you a future? How can I be the husband you deserve when I don't know how many tomorrows there will be?'

'And how can you not?'

There was a simplicity to her question, clarity that cleared the littered way for him.

'Rico, there are no guarantees in life; we've both learnt that the hard way. But if you love me as much as I love you then there can be no question of you walking away, no question of you dealing with this alone. I'd rather face the rest of my life without you, knowing I had one tiny slice when you were truly mine, than face a world without you ever having loved me at all.'

'I've always loved you, Catherine…' She heard his pause, knew there was more to come, but she shook her head and this time it was her finger hushing him with the softest of touches.

There was nothing left to qualify.

No words were needed now.

Love would see them through.

EPILOGUE

'I REALLY don't think you have anything to worry about. I know the books say that at this age toddlers can be very jealous of a new baby, but you must remember that Lily's very advanced.'

Antonia's voice carried across the veranda table and Catherine smothered a smile as Rico caught her eye.

'She is,' Antonia insisted. 'Anyway, we'll make sure she doesn't have a moment alone to feel jealous. Your father and I can hardly wait to have her stay with us.' She shot a rather impatient look across the table and this time Catherine didn't try to smother her smile; in fact, she threw her head back and laughed.

'I'm not due for another two weeks yet, Antonia. And, given the fact that first babies often come late, you might be in for a wait before Lily comes and stays with you.'

Selecting a strawberry from the fruit platter, Catherine bit into it, enjoying the sweet ripe taste, enjoying this lazy Saturday afternoon with her family by her side and a glimpse of the exciting times that lay ahead, and trying not to spoil this precious time with the pensive mood that had taken her today.

'Maybe Lily should have a trial run?' Rico's voice was so casual, his stance so nonchalant anyone else would have missed the meaning behind his words, and Catherine's eyes darted nervously to Antonia, watching the older woman's reaction as Rico's words hit home. 'Maybe she should go home with you both tonight?'

'You mean it?' Antonia didn't wait for an answer, scooping Lily up in her arms, ordering Carlos to load the car and showering her beloved granddaughter with kisses as Catherine packed an overnight bag. She slipped in a couple of bedtime stories for Carlos to read to her, albeit slowly. But *Three Little Ducks* was somehow so much more romantic with a Sicilian accent, and Lily was eternally patient, delighting in her doting grandfather's efforts, the perfect audience as he falteringly discovered the joy of reading.

'You've made their day.' Catherine sighed as they waved them off, leaning back on Rico, resting her head against his chest as his hands cupped her swollen stomach.

'It's the right thing to do,' Rico murmured, more to himself than to Catherine. 'Anyway, I had an ulterior motive. Do you realise this is probably our last night alone for a very, very long time?'

'Night feeds, dirty nappies.' Catherine sighed again. 'Are you sure you're ready to do it all again?'

'More than ready,' Rico affirmed. 'Aren't you?'

She was! Oh, for a while she'd been scared to glimpse the future. Rico's multitude of tests had consumed them, brave words no barrier against fear, but they had faced it together. Dark times were so much easier shared, and the blessed relief of a clean bill of health was so much sweeter with a family beside you.

'I'm ready, Rico.' She nestled against him, forcing herself to continue, forcing herself to share what was in her mind, as they had promised each other they would—only Rico got there first.

'Just not today, huh?'

'Just not today,' Catherine whispered back, grateful for his insight, and glad, so glad, she didn't have to hide her feelings any more.

'I've got something for you,' Rico said solemnly, turning her around to face him, pulling a piece of paper out of his pocket and handing it to her with trembling hands. 'I know it's going to make you cry, but it's something I think you should have—something I think *we* should have.'

She stared at the paper for an age and Rico was right, it did make her cry—but then every thing made her cry at the moment. Since Rico had switched on her emotions the world seemed to be a vivid contrast of delicious highs and lows, and she relished the rollercoaster she rode alongside him.

Somehow she even managed to relish standing in their courtyard on a Saturday afternoon, remembering the child they had lost one year ago on this day.

'I named a star.' Rico's voice wavered as he spoke and she waited patiently for him to continue. 'It *was* meant to be, Catherine. Our baby brought us together, made us the family we are today, and though I couldn't see it at the time I can see it so very clearly now. Our baby had a purpose.'

It was the most beautiful thing he could have said, the most beautiful thing anyone could have said, and as he took her hand and led her back to the house—a house that was now a home, filled with love, blessed with their beautiful Lily and a new baby soon to follow—Catherine knew the future was there for the taking, and that she was the luckiest woman in the world.

Tonight, though, was for them.

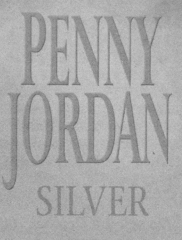

A story of passions and betrayals...
and the dangerous obsessions they spawn

PENNY
JORDAN
SILVER

Lynne
Graham
International Playboys

*Mistress and
Mother*

4 FREE

BOOKS AND A SURPRISE GIFT!

We would like to take this opportunity to thank you for reading this Mills & Boon® book by offering you the chance to take FOUR more specially selected titles from the Modern Romance™ series absolutely FREE! We're also making this offer to introduce you to the benefits of the Reader Service™—

- ★ **FREE home delivery**
- ★ **FREE gifts and competitions**
- ★ **FREE monthly Newsletter**
- ★ **Exclusive Reader Service offers**
- ★ **Books available before they're in the shops**

Accepting these FREE books and gift places you under no obligation to buy, you may cancel at any time, even after receiving your free shipment. Simply complete your details below and return the entire page to the address below. You don't even need a stamp!

YES! Please send me 4 free Modern Romance books and a surprise gift. I understand that unless you hear from me, I will receive 6 superb new titles every month for just £2.69 each, postage and packing free. I am under no obligation to purchase any books and may cancel my subscription at any time. The free books and gift will be mine to keep in any case.

P4ZED

Ms/Mrs/Miss/Mr ....Initials ....

BLOCK CAPITALS PLEASE

Surname ....

Address ....

....

....Postcode..................................

Send this whole page to:
UK: FREEPOST CN81, Croydon, CR9 3WZ